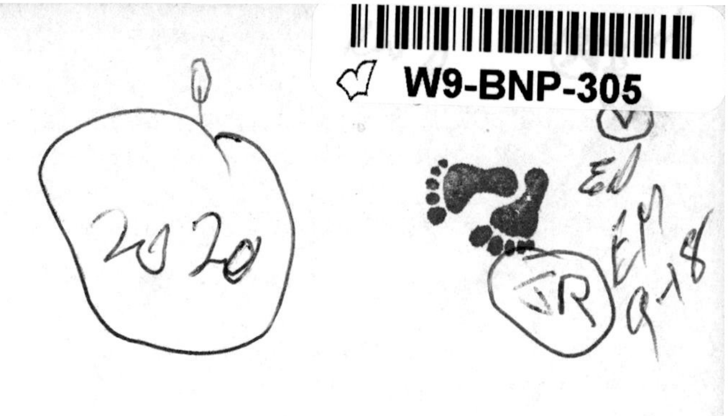

THE MAN THEY COULDN'T HANG

Marshal Lincoln Hawk rode into Independence hell-bent on finding the man who had gunned down his old friend Sheriff Ben Pringle, but within hours of arriving in town the saloon burns down, a businessman loses everything in a crooked poker game and Lincoln is fighting to save his own life against an unknown assailant. He suspects that one man may be responsible for all these incidents and that an old photograph might just hold the key to uncovering who he is. The trouble is, all the evidence points to the culprit being a man who was hanged ten years ago!

British Library Cataloguing in Publication Data.

Connor, Scott
The man they couldn't hang.

A catalogue record of this book is
available from the British Library

ISBN 978-1-84262-712-9 pbk

First published in Great Britain in 2007 by
Robert Hale Limited

Published in Large Print 2010 by arrangement with
Robert Hale Limited

Dales Large Print is an imprint of Library Magna Books Ltd.

Printed and bound in Great Britain by
T.J. (International) Ltd., Cornwall, PL28 8RW

The Man They Couldn't Hang

by

Scott Connor

Dales Large Print Books
Long Preston, North Yorkshire,
BD23 4ND, England.

PROLOGUE

The skull man was out there somewhere, and Sheriff Ben Pringle was waiting for him.

Ben rocked back and forth on his chair, the steady creak of the wooden runners beating an insistent rhythm on the porch. Beyond the bluff that stood before his house was the town of Independence and to his side was the wide expanse of the river that flowed around the town, its gentle gurgling coming to him on a light summer breeze. It was a pleasant evening, but it would later be marred by death.

Ben's eyes darted from side to side, looking out for the return of his Nemesis. A half-empty whiskey bottle was at his side. The consumed half had helped to keep his fear at bay, the unconsumed half remained in the bottle to keep his senses just sharp enough for him to react when he needed to. On his lap was an old photograph and dangling from his hand was his Peacemaker, loaded and ready for the skull man's arrival.

Ben had first seen him three months ago. He'd come from the direction of the river shortly after sundown and had stood watching the house from 400 yards away, a silent and enigmatic figure, not moving until Ben had left the house to approach him. Then he had melted into the gathering darkness.

A week had passed before he'd come again. He had again stood watching the house from the same position until the darkness had shrouded his form.

This time Ben hadn't reacted, contented just to watch him, and as if in response to Ben's lack of reaction the figure had become bolder. Every time he had subsequently appeared he had come closer and closer to the house.

Ben had resisted the urge to approach him and so give him the satisfaction of gaining the reaction he clearly wanted, but then the man had suddenly changed his policy. Ben had awoken in the middle of the night and had seen the man looking at him through the window. And in the harsh moonlight he'd seen the man's face, or lack of one. It appeared to be a skull staring unseeingly at him, pale and deathly beneath his lowered hat.

Half-thinking the vision had been a nightmare, Ben had stumbled to the window.

When he had looked out the figure had gone. But when he'd hurried outside and searched around he had found footprints for the first time and Ben had known this ghost was real. More important, when he'd accepted the vision wasn't a dream he realized where he'd seen a face like that before. For the next hour he'd ransacked his house until at the bottom of a cupboard he'd found the old photograph and he'd known who the skull man was.

But that man was dead.

In a desperate state he'd written a letter to the only person who he'd thought could help him, even if that person was the worst possible person from whom he could seek help. Afterwards he'd regretted his moment of weakness and had vowed to stop this man's haunting presence alone. Since then he had rarely slept, rarely eaten, and rarely gone into town, leaving his deputy to deal with routine matters as he'd awaited the skull man.

A week had now passed since the last sighting and something in Ben's guts, perhaps an old lawman's instincts, had told him that tonight was the night he would return.

The sun had set behind the bluff and

twilight darkness was enveloping the plains when he saw him. He was standing as he had done the first time he'd come, silent and still some 400 yards away and looking at the house.

Ben felt a twinge of disappointment. The man had been getting braver and he'd expected him to come closer to the house, but this appearance had returned to the manner of his first visitation.

Ben slipped the photograph into his pocket and, with his gaze set firmly on the figure, he walked to the front of his porch. It was still light enough to see for miles and the terrain around the figure was flat. If the man were to run, it would be hard for Ben and his ageing legs to catch up with him, but it would also be hard for the man to disappear quietly as he had done before.

'I'm going to get you this time,' Ben whispered to himself He fixed his total attention on the figure, ensuring he wouldn't let him out of his sight until he had him. 'We're just going to take this one step at a time.'

Ben paced off the porch and took his first step towards the figure, but then hot fire punched him deep in the guts, knocking him back a pace and into the porch post. He twisted round it, delayed shock letting him smell his own blood and hear the blast of the gunfire as he slid to the ground.

His vision was already darkening as he rolled onto his side, feeling the life-blood seep out of him. Even from the ground he could see the figure, looking at him. He couldn't have shot me from that distance, Ben thought to himself, his lawman's mind turning to resolving the reason behind the unexpected turn of events even as he felt the unending sleep of the dead overcome him.

His last sight before his vision departed for ever was the figure turning away and heading for the river with his shoulders slumped, and Ben's last, comforting thought was that he did appear disappointed.

CHAPTER 1

'Where did you find his body?' US Marshal Lincoln Hawk asked.

'Over there,' Deputy Alan Curtis said. He took a pace off the porch, then pointed to the ground. 'He was on his back with his gun at his side.'

Lincoln turned to stand with his back to the wall so he could look away from the house, as Sheriff Ben Pringle would have done just before he'd been murdered. It was a quiet location, ideal for a man who enjoyed his privacy, but making it unlikely that Lincoln would find any witnesses.

The sheriff had died a week ago and with the killer leaving no clues the investigation had stalled before it could make any progress. So Mayor Paul Ellison had called in Lincoln, a man with both the skills and the personal motivation to work out what had happened.

Lincoln had needed no encouragement to come to Independence and find out who had killed his old friend. Admittedly, he hadn't seen Ben for several years, but the anguish he'd felt on hearing the news was as great as if he'd seen him only yesterday. From that moment the determination to bring the culprit to justice had burned in his veins.

He'd arrived in town this morning and visiting the scene of the crime was his first act. His last would be bringing the killer to justice.

'Any known enemies?' he asked.

'The sheriff was popular,' Curtis said. 'I've been his deputy for a year and I can tell you in all that time he never made a single enemy.'

Lincoln snorted in disbelief. Lawmen made plenty of enemies. The fact he'd died with his gun drawn but not fired implied an organized assault from someone with a grudge who had sneaked up on him, but who had only alerted him at the last moment.

'Then any recent incidents that'll give me some suspects to start with?'

'Like I say – nope.'

'What about the town's known troublemakers?'

Curtis rubbed his bristled chin. 'The Humboldt brothers are behind most of the crime that goes on around here.'

Lincoln nodded. 'The mayor's already mentioned Karl Humboldt.'

'Yeah. Karl is the worst of the bunch and he was the first one I pulled in to question, but the trouble is, he and his brothers have solid alibis. They were drinking in the Golden Star saloon when the news came in about someone hearing gunfire out here.'

'Then whom did Ben arrest recently?'

'Aside from Karl there weren't many of them...' Curtis sighed and leaned on the rail to look out beyond the porch. When he spoke his voice was clipped and irritated. 'Sheriff Pringle wasn't himself recently. He'd taken to drinking heavily. For the last few months he drank with a kind of fanatical devotion. He used to throw the whiskey down his throat until he passed out, as if he wanted to forget something.'

Lincoln joined Curtis in leaning on the rail. 'I assume you have no idea what he was trying to forget?'

'No. Most days he looked like a haunted man who'd seen a ghost, but he didn't want to talk about it.'

Lincoln didn't believe in ghosts, but he did believe that some men and some grudges refused to lie down and die.

'Where did he drink?'

'Always in the Golden Star saloon, until he got too drunk and ornery and Wesley would refuse to serve the old whiskey hound.'

Lincoln snorted. 'Obliged for the answer, but don't speak ill of Ben again. I remember him when he was a fine man. Don't matter to me if his last months weren't his best. I'll find the man who killed him.'

With that promise made, Lincoln pushed himself from the rail. He looked at the chair by the door, remembering Ben sitting there, whistling contentedly as he enjoyed the last of the evening's light. That's where he'd been the last time he'd seen him and Lincoln resolved to always remember him that way.

'But how will you do that?' Curtis said, interrupting Lincoln's thoughts. 'There are no clues, no suspects, no way to even start–'

'I'll find him,' Lincoln snapped. 'Never doubt that for a moment.'

Lincoln stepped back to survey the scene of the murder, looking for any details that Deputy Curtis had missed. Lincoln had known the deputy for only a few hours but already he was getting the feeling that he wasn't particularly enthusiastic or competent. But before he could complete his search Curtis coughed to draw his attention, then pointed. Lincoln turned and saw a rider galloping through the scrub towards him.

'That's Malcolm Wilson,' Curtis said, 'owns the Bar W downriver.'

Lincoln left the house to meet him and the first thing he noticed was Malcolm's grim expression as he drew up his horse.

'You be the marshal?' Malcolm asked.

'Sure,' Lincoln said. 'What's the problem?'

'I've found a body.' Malcolm pointed to the river.

Lincoln glanced at Curtis and offered a grim smile.

'Now what were you saying about there being no clues?'

Curtis didn't reply other than to mutter under his breath, his eyes squinting with what Lincoln reckoned was annoyance.

Twenty minutes later they stood on the side of the river, some three miles downstream from Pringle's house.

'From the state of him,' Malcolm Wilson said, wrinkling his nose with distaste, 'I reckon he's been in the water for some time.'

Lincoln looked down at the corpse which had become entangled in a tree that had fallen into the river. A skeletal arm protruded above the head, bent backwards at an extreme angle and caught amongst the branches. The rest of the body was lying in the shallow water with the ragged clothes billowing on the surface and rippling in the gentle current. During his fifteen years of being a lawman Lincoln had seen some terrible sights and this was one of the worst.

Lincoln also felt a twinge of disappointment. He'd hoped that the body and Ben's murder might have an obvious link, but he was no longer sure. The dead man didn't appear to have fallen into the river, or to have been dumped there, but to have floated downstream, probably for some distance.

'How did you come across it?' Lincoln asked.

'I was watering my horse and there he was, just lying there in the water all dead.'

'If it weren't for the clothes, I couldn't say for sure it even was a man.'

Malcolm nodded. 'With his face all eaten away like that, guess it'll be hard to work out who he was.'

Lincoln turned to Curtis who was holding on to their horses.

'Come on, Curtis,' he said. 'I could do with some help getting him out of the water.'

Curtis raised his heels to look down into the water then shuddered and gripped the reins more tightly.

'I'll stay here and keep the horses under control,' he said with a rare show of determination, then fixed his gaze on the horses with a slow swing of his head. 'I don't want them getting spooked.'

The excuse was a poor one, but given the circumstances Lincoln couldn't blame him for distancing himself from what would be a hideous task. That didn't change the fact that he had to get the corpse out of the water, so he turned to Malcolm.

'In that case, Malcolm,' he said. 'I could do with your help.'

Malcolm winced, then provided a pronounced gulp.

'I was afraid you were going to ask me that,' he murmured.

Ten minutes later the body, wrapped in a horse-blanket, was on the back of Curtis's horse and the two lawmen were heading back to Independence, leaving a decidedly green-looking Malcolm behind them.

'What you reckon happened to him?' Lincoln asked.

'It's not my problem,' Curtis said, shrugging. 'He's been in the water for a while, so he might have come all the way down from beyond Black Point and that's out of my territory.'

'Perhaps he did, but I reckon he died at least a week ago – around the same time that Ben died.'

The possibility of there being a link didn't interest Curtis and he just delivered an irritated grunt. As they rode along he continued to grumble – as he had done since Lincoln had arrived in Independence. Whether this was because he didn't like his authority being usurped by Lincoln's presence, or because that was his nature, Lincoln didn't know. Although this time the wet and rotting smell coming from behind him gave him good cause for his complaints.

When they arrived back in town they drew up outside the undertaker's.

'Horses ain't looking spooked now,' Lincoln said. 'Get the body inside.'

'All on my own?' Curtis muttered, sneering.

'Yeah, on your...' Lincoln trailed off, finally letting his irritation at Curtis's surly attitude wear him down. 'Just do as I say and quit complaining.'

'I ain't got to do what no US Marshal says,' Curtis snapped back, waving his arms.

'I was Sheriff Pringle's deputy and I took his orders, but he ain't around no more to tell me what to do.'

'It's my investigation.' Lincoln lowered his voice to a growl. 'And you'll respect Ben's memory by following my orders.'

Curtis firmed his jaw, anger widening his eyes.

'You're right,' he grunted. 'It is your investigation. So you deal with the body.'

With that statement of defiance Curtis jumped down from his horse and headed off down the road towards the law office.

'Yeah,' Lincoln said to himself as he watched him leave, 'this is my investigation and the likes of you won't stop me completing it.'

CHAPTER 2

When Lincoln had dealt with the body he followed Curtis to the law office.

Curtis was sitting at his desk with his feet raised and his hat pulled down over his eyes. The deputy didn't acknowledge him, but Lincoln reckoned he didn't need his help right now and for the next few hours he searched through Sheriff Pringle's records. Unfortunately, they were as incomplete and useless as Lincoln had feared.

Ben had made few arrests recently, although the petty crime that usually went on in small towns continued unabated. Despite the lack of leads, one name appeared frequently, that of Karl Humboldt.

This evening Lincoln was due to attend a meeting with the mayor and other important townsfolk where he'd be able to learn more about what had been happening in town recently. That left him with several hours free, and the question of whether Karl had been involved in Ben's murder after all was the first subject he decided to tackle.

He headed over to Curtis's desk and stood looking down at him. Curtis squirmed, suggesting he knew Lincoln was watching him, but he said nothing.

'All right, Curtis,' Lincoln said. 'The two of us ain't got on well so far, but it's time we started working together on this.'

Curtis raised his hat with a finger and considered him while he flexed his jaw, making an obvious show of suppressing a yawn.

'Ain't got nothing to work on. Like I told you we got no clues, no leads, nothing.'

'Then we find some, and we'll start with Karl Humboldt.'

Curtis snorted. 'As I told you, he's got himself a solid alibi. He was drinking in the Golden Star saloon.'

'Then we'll check out that story in full, and the best person to start with is Wesley Jameson.' Wesley was the owner of the Golden Star saloon. 'Unless you already have a signed statement from him.'

'I guess,' Curtis murmured, casting a guilty glance at his feet, 'I forgot to talk to him.'

This revelation of incompetence didn't surprise Lincoln, and he limited himself to a mild admonishing sigh.

'Wesley should have been the first person

you talked to.' He set off for the door and held it open for Curtis, who took his time in swinging his legs down to the floor, lumbering across the office, and following him out.

'This is a waste of time if you ask me,' Curtis grumbled, this comment initiating a litany of complaints as they headed down the boardwalk.

Lincoln ignored him, having already heard most of the complaints at least once before.

The saloon wasn't open yet and so Lincoln peered through the window, cupping a hand beside his eyes to ward off the strong afternoon glare as he looked for signs of life inside. He flinched backwards, startled.

Inside, flickering flames were eating their way across the floor and heading towards the bar, the motion of the flames so swift that they appeared to be taking the path of gunpowder or perhaps spilt liquor.

At his side Curtis broke off from his complaints to bleat out a one-word cry.

'Fire!' Curtis turned on his heel and hurried off down the road screaming. 'Fire! Fire!'

Lincoln hurried to the door and kicked open the batwings, knocking one of them off its hinges. The rising heat from inside blasted his face, making him feel that his eyebrows were in danger of being singed. Even so, he edged forward another pace, an arm raised to his brow to shield his eyes from the raging heat. But the flames were advancing across the floor towards him with dangerous intent, already blocking off his path into the building. Worse, they were now licking at the barrels of liquor on the bar, something that was sure to have a disastrous effect. He backed away and out of the door, then pressed himself to the wall. He saw that Curtis had alerted a growing band of townsfolk who were hurrying down the road.

Mayor Ellison joined the group and quickly organized the townsfolk into lines to ferry then hurl water at the saloon. After a minute of frantic activity the water-carriers started to have an effect and killed the flames that had been licking around the doorway and windows.

Lincoln joined the mayor.

'Paul,' he shouted over the rising hubbub of alarm from the assembled townsfolk, 'have you seen Wesley?'

'Nope,' Ellison said. He glanced around until he saw Billy Stone, a saloon regular, then beckoned for him to join them and asked him the same question.

'Me neither,' Billy said. He removed his hat and crumpled it before him. 'I ain't seen him all day.'

With a sickness invading his guts, Lincoln looked at the flames until the heat watered his eyes and forced him to look away. From what he had heard of Wesley he was an obstinate man who was likely to have stayed inside in a futile attempt to save the building, even at the risk of the fire trapping him inside.

Lincoln located Deputy Curtis and patted his shoulder.

'Come on, Alan,' he said. 'We have to try and get in there.'

Curtis gave a reluctant nod and trudged after Lincoln. As they fought their way through the gathering crowd of helpers, Lincoln noticed something he hadn't seen before. Flames were licking at the front of the building, yet the back was relatively unscathed. Lincoln turned to pass this information on to Curtis, but Curtis had taken the opportunity of Lincoln's being temporarily distracted to slink away and was loitering before the nearest window where the water-throwers had fought back the flames.

Then a gout of flame burst through the door as a liquor barrel exploded, crashing the remaining burning batwing to the ground. Curtis scampered away, knocking over the two men behind him. And as all three men scurried away to a safer distance, Lincoln judged that if Wesley were inside, then explaining his thoughts would take up time that Wesley just didn't have.

So Lincoln ran in a wide half-circle around the saloon to reach the back and sure enough the rear exit was still free from flames, although huge swathes of smoke were spewing out of the door and windows.

Lincoln drew a kerchief from his pocket and wrapped it over his mouth. He looked around, judging the best way of approaching the building, and to the side he saw a man running away. Lincoln looked at his fleeing form, wondering if it were Wesley, but then another barrel in the saloon exploded, blasting a ball of flame through the back window.

In self-preservation, Lincoln dived to the ground with his arms over his head. Then inch by inch he looked up. He waited while he judged whether that explosion might herald a series of blasts and when several seconds had passed without a second explosion coming he jumped to his feet.

He saw that the blast had also knocked the running man to the ground. He saw him right himself, thrust his head down, and speed away, disappearing down the alley between the bank and Billy Stone's mercantile. Then movement in the saloon's back doorway drew his attention.

He blinked, clearing his watery gaze, and realized that he was seeing someone stagger into the doorway then fall to his knees. The man was plump and was clearly Wesley Jameson.

Lincoln set off and sprinted to the doorway. He skidded to a halt beside Wesley, who was conscious enough to mutter something, although his words were inaudible. He was clutching a burnt photograph to his chest and he kept his eyes tightly closed as smoke spiralled away from his clothing.

Wesley collapsed, but Lincoln grabbed him before he hit the ground. Then he shoved his hands under Wesley's armpits and walking backwards dragged him away from the saloon. Only when he was fifty yards away did Lincoln decide they were far enough away to be safe and lowered Wesley to the ground.

Lincoln batted Wesley's jacket, knocking

the glowing embers from his clothing, then rolled back on his haunches to watch Curtis hurry around the side of the saloon. He hailed the deputy with a wave, then pointed down at Wesley.

With his face wreathed in the first smile Lincoln had seen, Curtis joined him and slapped him on the back. Then Curtis knelt beside Wesley.

'You all right, Wesley?' he said.

Wesley rolled himself to his knees and cracked his watering eyes open to look at the burning saloon. He staggered on to all fours, dragged himself a clawed foot nearer, then slumped to the ground.

'Everything I had is gone,' he whined between coughs. He raised a hand. Clutched in it was the photograph. Half of it had blackened to ashes and as Lincoln watched the burnt half crumbled then fell away.

Wesley pressed his forehead to the ground and spluttered out a bout of hacking coughs.

'At least you still got your life,' Lincoln said. He placed a comforting hand on Wesley's back, but Wesley flinched away from him, then lay on his side and curled up into a ball as he watched the flames and smoke spiral up into the sky. His chest heaved with barely suppressed coughs.

'I've lost everything,' he croaked, then looked at the photograph, 'everything.'

Lincoln joined Wesley in looking at the burning building and although Wesley had clearly been talking about his saloon, Lincoln had the distinct impression he had meant the photograph.

'Curtis,' he said, pointing, 'get him to Doc Thoreau.'

'On my own?' Curtis grumbled.

'Yeah,' Lincoln said, heading away.

'And what're you doing?'

Lincoln didn't waste time explaining himself to the continually complaining and inefficient deputy and hurried on to the alley beside the bank. Someone had been running away from the fire and Lincoln resolved to find out why.

Nobody was in the alley, and so Lincoln headed down it to come out on the road beyond. To his right the townsfolk were helping out with the bucket-ferrying operation, and to his left Lincoln saw a man hurry behind the stables, the last building on the road on this side of town. The person was slim and possibly the man he'd seen earlier. With every person in town gravitating towards the fire, someone going in the opposite direction was unusual and intriguing.

Lincoln hurried across the road and rounded the corner of the stables to be greeted with the sight of the person he'd followed hunched over a hole a few yards away. From the description Curtis had given him earlier he identified him as being Alex Humboldt, the youngest brother of the notorious Humboldt clan.

'What you doing, Alex?' Lincoln said.

Alex flinched, then kicked out, knocking something that had been hidden behind his legs into the hole, the object landing with a clatter. He swirled round and offered a nervous smile.

'Nothing, I ain't doing nothing.'

Alex's efforts to hide whatever he'd been about to bury was such an obvious and pathetic attempt at subterfuge that Lincoln couldn't help but smile. Then his smile died when he noticed the top of the object poking out of the hole. It was a lamp.

He joined Alex and looked down into the hole, seeing that the lamp was broken. A glance at Alex's hands confirmed they were coated in oil. Lincoln gave a sorry shake of the head. Then with a casual gesture he reached out to Alex's top pocket and removed the matches he was sure would be there.

'Now, Alex,' he said, clamping a firm hand on his shoulder. 'You are under arrest.'

'What for?'

Lincoln took a significant glance at the broken lamp, Alex's oil-stained hands, then the matches before sniffing at the acrid smoke that was spreading around town.

'Arson, if Wesley lives. One hell of a lot worse if he doesn't. Perhaps plenty more than that if you don't co-operate.'

'But it wasn't me who torched the saloon.'

Lincoln noted that Alex appeared to have admitted he knew the fire wasn't an accident.

'Then who did?'

Alex gave a pronounced shiver. 'It was that man with the skull for a face.'

'The man with the skull for a face,' Lincoln intoned, letting his scepticism show in his pronounced sneer.

'Yeah. He had this face that...' Alex trailed off as Lincoln fixed him with his disbelieving gaze. 'I suppose you won't believe me. You'll just have to arrest me.'

'Already have, Alex,' Lincoln said as he dragged Alex off to the sheriff's office. 'Only question on my mind now is what else you and your brothers have been doing.'

CHAPTER 3

'How are you feeling?' Lincoln asked.

'Not good,' Wesley Pearson croaked. 'I just want to … to…'

A coughing fit cut short his statement.

It was early evening and although the townsfolk had stopped the fire spreading to the neighbouring buildings, the saloon had burnt to the ground and the cloying reek of burning was permeating the town. Doc Thoreau had set up a bed in his living-room for Wesley to rest on as he had nowhere else to stay.

Earlier, Lincoln had questioned Alex Humboldt and tried to poke holes in his story, but the young man had kept resolutely to his version of events.

He had seen a man running away from the burning saloon, followed him, and seen him putting the lamp in a hole. He'd surprised the man and when he'd turned to look at him, the man appeared to have a skull for a face. Then this person had run away and when Alex had picked up the lamp he'd found that it was broken and it had leaked oil over his hands.

Alex's story didn't explain why he had kicked the lamp into the hole or why he'd acted so guiltily. Although from what Curtis had told him, any member of the Humboldt family usually had a reason to look guilty.

Lincoln was prepared to dismiss Alex's sighting of the skull as being a trick of the light, but not the possible presence of an unidentified man, who had apparently set fire to the saloon. Whether Alex was telling the truth or not, Lincoln had a hunch the fire was connected to the Humboldt brothers' claim that they had been drinking there on the night of Ben's murder.

So Lincoln had discussed the arrest with Judge Murphy, but the judge had reckoned that unless he obtained better evidence that Alex couldn't easily explain away he'd have no choice but to release him. With this in mind, Wesley was Lincoln's last hope of keeping Alex in a cell.

'That's enough questions, Lincoln,' Doc Thoreau said, shaking his head. 'He needs rest.'

'And he'll get it, but I need information. Just tell me quickly, Wesley. Did you see who burnt down your saloon?'

Wesley shook his head, the action making him wheeze then fall back on to the bed with pain contorting his face.

'Did you see Alex Humboldt?'

'I...' Wesley coughed and spluttered, his face going bright red with the effort of trying to talk.

'Did you–?'

'Enough!' Thoreau said, raising his voice and shaking an admonishing finger at Lincoln.

Lincoln still had several questions he wanted to ask, but he was getting the feeling he wouldn't receive an answer to any of them. Whether Wesley was overemphasizing the amount of pain he was in to avoid answering or he was really that ill, Lincoln couldn't tell. With Thoreau giving him no choice, he relented and left Wesley's bedside, but at the door he stopped and slipped in one final question.

'Did you see the Humboldt brothers in your saloon on the night Ben Pringle died?'

'No,' Wesley said, his quick response sounding confident before he looked aloft, his brow furrowing with thought, then continued. 'At least I... I...'

Another bout of coughing stopped him from continuing with his answer and with

Thoreau muttering with displeasure and pointing at the door, Lincoln left. Thoreau stayed behind to check on Wesley, leaving Lincoln alone in the hall. Smiling with the thought that Karl Humboldt's alibi wasn't as strong as Deputy Curtis had claimed, Lincoln was about to head outside. Then he noticed Wesley's jacket lying over a chair. Poking out of a pocket was the corner of the burnt photograph Wesley had been clutching when he'd emerged from the burning saloon.

Lincoln went over to the chair to remove the photograph. When he saw what it depicted he was pleased he'd let his curiosity get the better of him.

'Interesting, isn't it?' Thoreau said, coming through the door.

Lincoln turned. 'Certainly confirms to me the fire is connected to Ben's murder. You mind if I take it?'

'I wouldn't. Wesley might, but I've given him something to make him sleep, so I doubt he'll object.' Thoreau pointed to the door. 'You going to the meeting now?'

'Sure.'

'Then pass on my apologies. I'll be there later.' Thoreau turned to his surgery. 'I've just received that body you fished out the river earlier. I'll see if I can find out anything about it before I come over.'

Lincoln acknowledged Thoreau's help with a curt nod then headed outside to find that Deputy Curtis was mooching around outside.

'What you doing here?' Lincoln asked.

'Nothing,' Curtis said. He cast a significant glance down the road while rocking from foot to foot.

'In that case I'll give you something to do. Get back to the law office, give Alex another hour to stew, then let him go, but follow him and see what he does.'

Lincoln set off for the Rising Sun saloon, but Curtis shuffled to the side to block his way.

'On my own?' he bleated, his eyes opening wide with shock.

Lincoln closed his eyes for a moment and breathed deeply to calm himself.

'Sure,' he said when he'd controlled his irritation. 'Why not?'

'Look.' Curtis pointed down the road with a shaking hand. 'The Humboldt brothers are here.'

Lincoln leaned forward to look down the road and eventually saw the reason for Curtis's furtive behaviour. Three surly-looking individuals were loitering on the other side of the road, eyeing the law office.

'Don't let the likes of them intimidate you. Follow Alex and if he rejoins his brothers, you can watch what they all do.' Lincoln slapped a firm hand on Curtis's shoulder. 'And if they confront you, it'll give you a chance to check their alibi.'

Curtis shrugged. 'What you mean?'

'I mean I've heard that Karl Humboldt wasn't in the Golden Star saloon on the night Ben died. You need to be more thorough when you check out people's stories.'

Curtis murmured a denial that didn't sound convincing but Lincoln ignored him and headed off down the road. From the corner of his eye he saw the brothers look his way then peel away from the wall to follow him. It was only a short distance across the road, but Lincoln walked slowly ensuring they could catch up with him before he reached the saloon.

He heard their steady footfalls filing in behind him and when he'd reached the batwings he stopped, then slowly turned. Karl Humboldt stood at the front of the bunch with the other two brothers, Heinrich and Wilhelm, behind him.

'Howdy,' Lincoln said, 'you'd be the older

Humboldt brothers. Don't leave town. I'll be having a word with you later.'

Karl opened his mouth as if to snap back a retort but then closed it, Lincoln's unconcerned and direct approach probably bemusing him.

'We're the ones who want a word with you,' he muttered. 'You've got our brother in a cell and he ain't done nothing wrong.'

'Don't waste your time worrying about him. He'll have company soon enough.'

Lincoln glared at Karl, then, just as Karl started to snap back a threat, he turned on his heel and headed inside. Without looking back he went up to the private room upstairs. He didn't hear them follow him in and he presumed they'd headed back down the road to resume their loitering outside the sheriff's office where they'd been goading each other on to do something.

Aside from Doc Thoreau, Lincoln was the last to arrive for his important meeting, the other four men already having taken their positions around the table. When he'd sat, Mayor Ellison gave a call for everyone to be quiet for a minute in remembrance of Sheriff Pringle, who couldn't be here for the first time ever. Then he got the meeting under way.

Two hours later Lincoln was fifteen dollars down and looking at yet another dull hand.

'Damn,' he murmured, as he fingered the useless three of diamonds Mayor Ellison had just dealt him.

Ellison chuckled. 'Sounds to me like you ain't enjoying taking Ben's place tonight.'

'I am.' Lincoln leaned back from the table and snorted. 'I'm just not enjoying the cards you're dealing me.'

The other poker-players laughed.

Since the founding of Independence, every month a poker-game had taken place in a private room at the back of the Golden Star saloon. The game attracted Independence's premier people: Wesley Jameson, Billy Stone, Judge Daniel Murphy, Doc Thoreau, Mayor Paul Ellison, and Sheriff Ben Pringle.

The stakes were low and the enthusiasm for the game of poker was equally low. But, from the tales Ellison had told Lincoln, the conversation was ripe, the drinking was heavy, and late into the night many important items of town politics had been decided upon and many new business opportunities had been discussed. But with the fire having destroyed the Golden Star saloon, the game was now taking place in the Rising Sun saloon at the opposite end of town.

Lincoln had taken Sheriff Pringle's place and as Wesley Jameson wasn't well enough to attend an opportunity had opened up and had gone to a dour traveller, Jack Porter. He was a quiet man who had what Lincoln reckoned was a studied routine of fingering his chin whenever he received a bad hand.

'It's important to keep up the tradition of always having a lawman present,' Judge Murphy said. 'It's a double benefit that you're an old friend of Ben's.'

Lincoln smiled, pleased that the judge had provided him with an opportunity to discuss the only subject on his mind, and the only reason he'd decided to spend a night playing poker when he had a killer to find.

'It must be hard on you all not to have Ben here.' Lincoln paused while everyone murmured their agreements. 'But I don't intend to be around this time next month. You'll have to find another lawman to take my place, like Deputy Alan Curtis.'

This comment raised several laughs.

'He isn't suitable for this evening,' Murphy said.

'Or anything else,' Doc Thoreau said, smiling.

Murmured agreements drifted around the table.

'Ben thought him suitable enough to be his deputy,' Lincoln said.

'And the reason why he thought that,' Thoreau said, 'is a mystery to us all. In the three months he's been in town, he's done nothing good.'

'Three months? Curtis said he'd been here for a year.'

'And that is precisely the sort of pointless lie that proves he wasn't fit to be a deputy to a man like Sheriff Ben Pringle.'

Lincoln waited while Ellison dealt out the remaining cards before speaking again.

'Anyone know why Ben was so depressed recently?'

Everyone but Jack shook their heads.

'He was worried about something, that's for sure,' Ellison said. 'And speaking of being depressed, maybe Alex's arrest will cheer up Wesley.'

'It won't,' Judge Murphy said. 'There no evidence he burnt down the saloon. I've already advised Lincoln to release him.'

'What about the lamp he was trying to bury?'

'Proves nothing. He could have found it like he said.'

Lincoln watched Ellison and Murphy knock the subject back and forth. The facts surrounding Alex's arrest ought to have been a private matter that only got an airing in the courthouse but in a small town news travelled fast no matter how private. Lincoln took note of what everyone said during their free and unguarded chatter, trying to understand the politics and personalities. He became particularly intrigued when Ellison veered the conversation away from the fire.

'Is Wesley still mooning over that photograph?' he asked, turning to Doc Thoreau.

'What photograph?' Billy Stone asked before Doc Thoreau could answer.

Ellison considered Billy. 'I've heard he risked staying in the saloon to save some photograph.'

Billy lowered his head, his narrowed eyes registering some emotion, perhaps surprise, as Lincoln glanced around the table, noting that everyone else was darting significant glances at each other. So he placed his cards on the table, face down, and slipped the photograph from his pocket.

'While Wesley was getting himself some

rest, I borrowed it,' he said, with a smile and a wink to Doc Thoreau.

Lincoln passed the photograph to Ellison, who jerked his head down to consider it over the top of his glasses. Judge Daniel Murphy craned his neck to see it, but Billy and Jack didn't move.

Only half the picture remained and on that half three men stood before a saloon, its sign not visible. There were no clues as to its location. One of the men was Wesley Jameson. The other man was Sheriff Pringle. Lincoln didn't recognize the third man.

'No idea where and when this was taken,' Ellison said, shrugging. 'It might have been when Ben and I were running for office. Why are you so interested in it?'

'Two people in that photograph have had bad fortune recently and I'm asking myself why.'

'If you're doing that,' Doc Thoreau said, 'you should note that two members of this poker-group have also had bad luck.'

Lincoln had already considered this possibility. He had also wondered whether other members of the group might be in the half of the picture that had been burnt away.

Ellison held out the picture to Judge Murphy.

'I don't reckon it's important, and none of us likes to hear of bad luck being contagious when we're playing poker.'

Lincoln looked at Judge Murphy. 'Do you know who the other man is?'

The judge and the mayor shot quick glances at each other that Lincoln couldn't help but notice before the judge replied.

'No.'

Doc Thoreau leaned over to take the photograph then stabbed a finger against the leg and partially displayed torso of a fourth figure that was protruding into the picture, the main bulk of his form being on the missing half

'That looks like you, Billy,' he said.

Billy snorted then snatched the picture from Thoreau's grasp. He glanced at it then shook his head and threw it on the table.

'That ain't me,' he said, sneering. 'Now, if our lawman has finished distracting us, I reckon it's my bet, and I raise fifty.'

Several grumbles sounded around the table, as Lincoln slipped the photograph back into his pocket.

'As you well know, the house limit is five dollars,' Ellison muttered, fingering his cards and glaring at Billy over the top of his glasses. 'You can't raise fifty.'

'I just did.' Billy licked his lips. 'But if you ain't got the guts to match me, you can carry on hiding behind your precious rules.'

Several people complained at once, shaking their heads or fingers as they registered their irritation. With Billy's outburst making everyone forget they'd been talking about Ben's death, the fire, and the photograph, Ellison snorted and slammed his cards to the table, face down.

'Damn it, Billy. It's always the same when you get a few whiskeys inside you. You get serious and our friendly game of poker comes to its usual argumentative end.'

Murphy muttered with irritation too, but just as he had done all evening, the newcomer Jack Porter sat quietly and steadily shuffled his cards back and forth. Murphy glanced at Jack, then at Lincoln.

'What you reckon, Marshal?' he asked. 'Do we stop Billy breaking the house limit or should one of us teach him the lesson he so richly deserves?'

'I reckon arrogance should always be beaten down,' Lincoln said. He twitched a smile, but then hurled his cards on the table face down. 'But to be honest, I ain't got the cards to teach anyone a lesson.'

Billy grunted with contentment. 'Ellison,

if you ain't man enough to match me either, throw your cards in too.'

Ellison smiled and placed his cards on the edge of the table. He stood, then turned and from the bottle on the cabinet behind him poured himself a good measure of whiskey.

'That's the difference between you and me, Billy.' He returned to the table. 'I don't play poker to win. I play to enjoy everyone's company.'

Prolonged laughter and guffaws emerged from every man, even the newcomer.

'In my experience, anyone who says they ain't playing to win is *only* playing to win.' Billy set his lips into a thin smile and peered at Ellison over the top of his cards. 'You in?'

Ellison prised up the corners of his cards to consider them, then shook his head and hurled them on top of Lincoln's.

'Nope. Got the same problem as Lincoln has.'

Billy looked at Murphy. 'And you?'

'I've got the cards, but I ain't locking horns with you if you're getting serious.' Murphy threw his cards on the pile. 'Five dollar limit is fine by me.'

With Doc Thoreau also throwing his cards in, Billy looked at Jack.

'And you, new man?'

Jack considered Billy with his jaw set firm and jutting. A finger rose to touch his chin, but then veered away as he gathered up a tangle of bills from his stash and patted them into a neat pile.

'So you're saying the five dollar limit no longer applies, are you?'

'Yep,' Billy said, 'for this one hand.'

'In that case, I'm in.' Jack threw the bills in the pot, receiving a wide grin from Billy. Then with his gaze set on Billy he reached into his pocket and extracted a billfold. 'And I'll raise you two hundred.'

'Well I'll be,' Ellison declared, tucking his thumbs in his waistcoat pockets. 'That'll teach you, Billy. You've been pulling that trick on us for years. It's about time someone paid you back.'

'Yep,' Murphy said, chuckling. 'I ain't losing sleep over someone fleecing you.'

Jack's expression remained as dour as it had been all night.

'Quit the banter,' he muttered. 'I want to hear what Billy has to say about my raise. Unless he's too yellow to play real poker.'

'Hey,' Ellison said, raising a hand. 'We may have argued with Billy, but this is a friendly game between friends. We have a few drinks, swap gossip, and enjoy our evening. We don't play real poker.'

'We might not,' Billy said, eyeing Jack with interest. 'But it ain't long past that I used to play real poker and I'm ready to play some now.' Billy drew a pen and an envelope from his pocket. With his head down, he scrawled a note on the envelope, signed it, then tossed it on the pot. 'I match your two hundred and raise you five hundred. That interest you, or are you too yellow to play real poker?'

As one, Ellison and Murphy slammed their hands over their eyes. Even Lincoln joined them in wincing.

'I ain't too yellow,' Jack said. He took the envelope Billy had scrawled on and added his own note below Billy's, then signed it and threw it back on the pot. 'And I reckon I'll pay to see you.'

Sporting a sly smirk, Billy laid down his cards. Combining with the two tens on the table he had a full house, aces over tens.

Jack glanced at his cards, then one at a time laid down his cards to reveal he had the remaining two tens.

Billy snorted, then lowered his head until his brow rested on the table. He massaged the back of his neck as he breathed deeply, then leaned back in his chair and forced a smile.

'Didn't think you could have both tens,' he murmured. His voice caught. 'That was the only hand that could beat mine.'

'It sure was a rare stroke of luck.' Jack glanced at Mayor Ellison, Judge Murphy, then Lincoln and Thoreau. 'You all witnessed our promises.'

'We're an honourable town,' Ellison said, leaning back in his chair to pat his rounded belly. 'Don't doubt for a moment that one of our citizens won't pay his debts.'

Jack tipped his hat. 'No offence meant.'

'None taken,' Ellison said. He glanced at Billy, then sighed and slapped his hands on his thighs. 'And on that note, I reckon that's my last hand tonight.'

Murphy murmured an agreement, Lincoln joining him.

'And what about you, Billy?' Jack said, placing a finger on the envelope. 'You had enough?'

'Yeah. Perhaps it has been too many years since I last played real poker. I reckon I'll quit.' Billy tipped his hat and scraped back his chair. 'You'll have to wait until morning for me to get the money from the bank.'

'I can do that, but it's a pity the game had to end so early. Perhaps if you were to stay, you might win your money back.' Jack placed another finger on the envelope then raised it and wafted it back and forth. 'Then you won't have to visit that bank tomorrow morning.'

Billy turned to file out through the door behind Ellison, but then stopped, looked aloft, and slowly turned back. Everyone looked at him, shaking their heads.

'Remember, Billy,' Doc Thoreau said, 'what Lincoln was saying earlier. Two members of this poker-group have had terrible luck recently.'

'Well,' Billy said, heading back to the table, 'perhaps it's about time I changed that luck.'

CHAPTER 4

In the morning Marshal Lincoln Hawk headed into the sheriff's office and considered Deputy Curtis.

'Enjoy your important meeting last night?' Curtis asked, his face hidden beneath his hat as he leaned back in his chair.

Lincoln provided a rueful grunt then went to the stove and poured himself a mug of coffee.

'You mean you haven't heard what happened?'

'Nope.' Curtis raised his hat, curiosity lighting his eyes as he rocked his feet down from his desk.

'Then in short, I didn't.' Lincoln swirled his coffee.

Curtis laughed. 'You couldn't have lost that much with their five-dollar limit, surely.'

Lincoln shrugged then headed over to Curtis's desk.

'I lost fifteen dollars.'

'That ain't much of a reason for such a long face.'

'It ain't what I lost that's depressing me. It was what Billy Stone lost.' Lincoln placed his coffee mug on Curtis's desk and folded his arms. 'This gambler Jack Porter took Wesley Jameson's place at the table and beat Billy for hand after hand.'

Curtis winced. 'How much did he win?'

'Twenty-five.'

'Twenty-five dollars!' Curtis laughed. 'Billy can afford that.'

'No, twenty-five thousand.'

Curtis's mouth fell open. For long moments he stared at Lincoln then blew out his cheeks as he glanced away.

'You're jesting.'

'Wish I were.' Lincoln sat on the edge of Curtis's desk and nursed his coffee mug. 'Worst streak of luck I've ever seen. Billy kept raising the stakes and Jack kept matching him and beating him. Billy figured that his luck had to change. But it didn't and by the time sense had descended on him, Jack had taken him for everything he had.'

Curtis blew out his cheeks. 'Trouble?'

'Nope. Billy was just too plumb distraught to complain.'

'I reckon Billy had it coming to him. I've always reckoned his talk of how he once took on the big city gamblers was probably just that – talk.'

'And if it was just talk, then last night it rode into town, chewed him up and spat him out.' Lincoln stood and headed to the window. He peered down the road at the burnt-out wreckage of the Golden Star saloon while sipping his coffee. 'Seems as if it's true. Independence's poker group ain't had much luck recently. First Ben Pringle gets murdered. Then Wesley Jameson loses everything. Now Billy Stone has too.'

Curtis shrugged. 'Trouble comes in threes. Let's hope that's it.'

'I ain't superstitious.' Lincoln turned and considered Curtis. 'And what did you find out when you followed Alex last night?'

'Ah,' Curtis murmured, not meeting Lincoln's eye, 'I didn't exactly... I lost him. He was too damn sneaky for me.'

Lincoln gulped down the last of his coffee to avoid saying that a dead rattler in a cage could probably have outfoxed Deputy Curtis.

'Luckily I'm sneakier than the likes of Alex Humboldt.' Lincoln opened the door and called over his shoulder as he headed outside. 'I'll see if Wesley is well enough to talk. You do ... do whatever it was you were doing.'

Curtis grunted with contentment, settled back in his chair, and drew his hat down over his eyes. Lincoln noted that sleeping was one of the few activities at which the deputy excelled.

Wesley was still staying with Doc Thoreau. Last night after the poker-game Lincoln had returned the half-photograph to Thoreau with a request that he sneak it back into Wesley's jacket. Although Wesley had still been too unwell to answer questions, Lincoln hoped this situation had now changed. But when he arrived at the doctor's house, Thoreau reported that Wesley was still resting and he didn't want Lincoln to disturb him.

'Sorry,' Lincoln said, 'I know you want Wesley to get as much rest as possible, but I have to question him some more now.'

Thoreau sighed. 'I guess it won't hurt, but do it quickly and don't get him agitated. He swallowed a lot of smoke.'

Thoreau beckoned Lincoln to follow him through to the living-room, but then stopped in the doorway. The room was empty. A tangled heap of blankets showed where Wesley had been having what was clearly his unsettled rest.

They searched the rest of the house, confirming that Wesley had gone. Although

Wesley's health was in a poor state, it didn't put him in any immediate danger, so neither man was too concerned as they headed outside and looked up and down the road.

They questioned each person who passed. Nobody had seen Wesley. Lincoln was about to head off to search for him when Thoreau reported that he had some promising news on the other matter to arise on the previous day. He beckoned for Lincoln to follow him and took him through to his surgery. On a table was the coffin containing the body Lincoln had fished out of the river. On another table lay a mouldering pile of clothes and beside it a smaller pile of objects. Thoreau pointed out a distorted slug.

'I got that out of his chest,' he reported.

Lincoln went over to the table and fingered the slug.

'So it was murder,' he mused.

Thoreau removed a photograph from the pile of belongings and gestured with it to get Lincoln's attention, then gave a slow and knowing nod.

'You also might find this interesting,' he said, passing the picture over to Lincoln. 'It's from the dead man's possessions.'

'Not another photograph,' Lincoln murmured as he took the picture.

'I don't reckon so. I reckon it's the same one.'

With his interest piqued Lincoln looked at the photograph. It was battered and faded, its time in the water and the rough treatment it'd received having worn away most of the picture that had once been there, but it appeared to depict seven people standing in a line.

Lincoln narrowed his eyes and hunched over the picture, trying to discern details of who the people were. Unfortunately, decay had faded their forms to blank ghosts, making their identification impossible, but when Lincoln recalled the half-picture, he reckoned that the people were standing in the same positions in both pictures.

'Why would a dead man I fished out the river have the same photograph on him as Wesley had?'

Thoreau shrugged. 'I'm just helping you to uncover the facts. You'll have to work that one out for yourself.'

'I wonder if Ben had another copy of this picture?'

'Good thinking, but I don't know. I'm not sure who got his property.'

Lincoln nodded. 'Perhaps one of the other men in the picture is the dead man.'

Thoreau glanced at the picture, an amused gleam in his eye.

'Now that is excellent thinking,' he said, then pointed at the ghostly image that was standing at the end of the line of people. 'I can't be certain but I reckon that man is Lenox Devere.'

'Lenox ... you worked out who the body was?'

'Sure did. It required deductive reasoning, plenty of hard work, and an eye for the fine detail that lesser men would miss.' Thoreau waited while Lincoln gave a congratulatory nod, then winked. 'And it helped that the body had an engraved cigarette case on it.'

Lincoln laughed. 'That doesn't have to be the dead man's despite your deductive reasoning and eye for the fine detail.'

'It doesn't, but I've heard of Lenox Devere. He was a nasty critter from up in Black Point. It doesn't surprise me that someone with as many enemies as he had ended up dead and floating down the river.'

'Did he know the Humboldt brothers?'

'Don't know.'

'Did Ben ever have a run-in with him?'

'I believe he did.' Thoreau shook his head as Lincoln registered his interest by raising an eyebrow. 'Not that I'm saying anything specific. I just know Ben went up to Black Point every month.'

'But you don't know why?'

'Nope.' Thoreau frowned, appearing almost apologetic for having raised a question of doubt without anything to back it up. 'Sorry. I've got nothing else to link Lenox's death to Ben's, other than...'

'Than just a hunch?' Lincoln said, completing the thought.

'Yeah. Somehow that–'

A gunshot blasted outside, the faint sound coming from some distance away. Both men hurried to the window. The few people outside were standing still, caught in that moment of indecision Lincoln had seen before where innocent people hear gunfire and want to run, but don't know in which direction to run. Then slowly and collectively people started to look towards the edge of town and the wreckage of the Golden Star saloon.

Lincoln and Thoreau exchanged a glance and a nod then hurried outside. They ran down the road towards the saloon. In the windows they passed faces appeared and craned their necks as they looked out to see what had happened, and Lincoln shouted out instructions for everyone to stay where they were.

With Thoreau two paces behind him, Lincoln bounded on to the burnt timbers of the boardwalk outside the saloon and together they peered through the blackened hole of the window.

Within the ruined building, the stray whiff of smoke still emerged from objects blackened beyond recognition, but aside from that, the room was still. Then from further inside a clatter sounded, as of something falling.

Lincoln pointed to the alley beside the saloon and with hand gestures told Thoreau to enter the building through the front door while he went in through the back.

Lincoln scurried down the alley and around the back of the saloon. He picked a route over the heaps of burnt and fallen timbers, many of which had been reduced to ash shadows, to stand on the spot where yesterday he had watched Wesley stagger out of the burning building. Then he slipped inside.

The saloon was small, the main room having comprised most of the building. With the fire having collapsed the internal walls, Lincoln could see into all four corners of the building. He ran his gaze over the charred remnants of Wesley's business, searching for movement.

From the front, Thoreau paced into the doorway and matched Lincoln's slow gaze around the ruined saloon.

Lincoln edged inside. After three paces he saw the only splash of colour within the building. After another pace he realized it was a leg that had sprawled out from behind the skeletal remains of the bar. He gestured to Thoreau, conveying that he'd seen something and the two men climbed over the heaps of burnt furniture and a length of collapsed roof to reach the bar.

With his teeth gritted in preparation for seeing what he reckoned he'd see, Lincoln peered over the bar and confirmed that the leg belonged to Wesley, who lay prone.

He stood aside as Thoreau slipped past him and rolled the body over. Wesley flopped over to lie on his back, his mouth wide open, the bullet wound that had ripped into the centre of his forehead showing he'd never share a friendly chat with anyone over a whiskey again. But Thoreau still hunkered down beside him and fingered his neck, then shook his head.

Lincoln noted that Wesley was clutching his copy of the burnt photograph, its image possibly being the last thing he'd seen before dying.

With his voice sounding gruff, Lincoln asked Thoreau to stay there while he checked out the rest of the building. Lincoln then paced around as much of the building as he dared, searching for any hidden assailant without risking the walls collapsing in on him.

They hadn't seen anyone running away from the building and so the killer could still be here. But the fire had reduced everything he touched to insubstantial ghosts that had the rigidity of powder, and there was nowhere where someone could hide. So he returned to find that Thoreau had pulled Wesley out from behind the bar and laid a singed cloth he'd found over his face. He was standing over the body with his hat tipped back, shaking his head.

'Don't blame yourself,' Lincoln said.

'I don't. Wesley was free to come and go as he pleased.'

Lincoln patted Thoreau's shoulder then looked around the saloon with his hands on his hips. He sighed, pondering on recent events while taking deep breaths to clear his lungs of the lingering taint of burning and death.

Movement caught his eye and he glanced

to the side, then stumbled back in shock. A man was looking at him through the blackened gap of the saloon's back window. The window was high in the wall and so Lincoln could only see his body above shoulder-height. The man had his hat pulled low and the face that peered out from beneath the hat was not that of a man. It appeared to be a skull, although Lincoln thought he caught the glimpse of eyes within the sockets.

'Thoreau,' he said, turning to him. 'Who's that?'

'Who's what?' Thoreau asked, looking around.

Lincoln pointed as he turned back but the man had gone, leaving silently as if he'd never been there, the sudden nature of his arrival and departure suggesting it'd been a vision. Lincoln had been thinking back to the fire and this along with Alex's cryptic comment about the man with a skull for a face added further credibility to this possibility.

'Do you believe in...?' Lincoln trailed off, unwilling to complete his question.

'You look spooked,' Thoreau said.

'I guess I am,' Lincoln said. 'Stay here with Wesley.'

Lincoln shook his head as he walked over to

the window, freeing his mind of its consideration of the sighting being a vision. Maybe later he would be prepared to accept that his over-active imagination had conjured up the vision of a man, but only after he'd exhausted the more rational explanation. He peered outside but saw nobody, then slipped out through the rear exit and looked back and forth. He still saw nobody and as he headed off towards the bank he considered.

Anyone who'd gone in the opposite direction and headed away from town would have had to pass the door and someone acting stealthily wouldn't have done that, so he had to have gone towards the bank. Lincoln stopped. If the person's escape route was the same as it'd been the previous night, he knew where he'd go. He doubled back, ran through the saloon, shouting out a quick instruction to Thoreau to alert Deputy Curtis, then hurried down the road to the stables.

At the stables he rounded the corner at a run and just caught a fleeting glimpse of a man disappearing around the next corner. Keeping his footfalls light he hurried to that corner and peered around the side, but saw nobody. Then he noticed that the back door to the stables was open.

With his gun held out before him he paced

to the door and looked inside. Five yards beyond, in the darkened interior, a man was standing with his back to him, looking around the stables. Lincoln wasted no time and paced up to him, his gun aimed at the small of the man's back.

The man continued to look around as Lincoln approached, then flinched, apparently suddenly realizing that Lincoln was closing on him. He started to turn and so in a rush Lincoln paced up to him. When the man completed his turn he found himself looking down the barrel of Lincoln's gun.

For his part, Lincoln had expected to be confronting the skull man, but found that he was facing the more familiar form of Alex Humboldt.

'What are you doing here?' Lincoln demanded.

'I was chasing after that man,' Alex said, his eyes darting about, perhaps in shock, or perhaps furtively. 'He was the same one that I saw yesterday. I thought he came in here, but perhaps he didn't.'

Lincoln might have been prepared to believe this statement if he hadn't seen the gun in Alex's hand, the blood on his jacket, and the startled look in Alex's eyes. Alex noticed Lincoln's interest and started to turn the gun on him, but Lincoln lunged out and flicked the weapon from Alex's grasp, then grabbed him.

'You are under arrest, Alex,' he said, 'again, and this time it's really serious.'

With an arm firmly clamped around Alex's shoulders he headed to the door and looked outside. Beyond was deserted countryside with no sign of anyone. He looked at Alex with his eyebrows raised.

Alex darted his gaze along the back of the row of buildings, seemingly searching for the man he had claimed to be following, then sighed and looked at Lincoln with beseeching eyes.

'The skull man was there, honestly. I was following him and he...' Alex kicked at the dirt then slumped his shoulders. 'I guess you'll just have to arrest me again.'

Lincoln nodded then turned to head off for the sheriff's office. He was minded to continue searching, but he was unwilling to do that with a prisoner in tow. Luckily, Deputy Curtis then arrived.

'You got here quickly for once,' Lincoln said.

Curtis shrugged. 'I heard gunfire and came running.'

Lincoln narrowed his eyes with scepticism. Curtis hadn't come out on to the road after the only gunshot. In his opinion the only direction Curtis was likely to run when he heard gunfire was in the opposite direction to the gunfire, but with the situation being urgent he kept those thoughts to himself. He passed Alex over to the deputy and after they'd set off for the sheriff's office he returned to the stables. His quick search revealed nothing untoward and so he headed outside, then along the backs of the buildings on the main road.

He still didn't see anybody, and when he returned to the main road the only people outside were the townsfolk who were gradually gathering around the saloon in a silent and sombre group.

In a small town like Independence any visitor gathered plenty of attention and a man with a face as distinctive as the face Lincoln had seen would be sure to gather interest.

Lincoln smiled as he connected the evidence in the only way possible. 'Either I'm seeing things,' he said to himself, 'or the skull man is a familiar face around town and he's wearing a mask.'

CHAPTER 5

News travelled fast in Independence, especially when the Humboldt brothers were involved. So when Lincoln left the courthouse after talking over the situation with Judge Murphy, the three free brothers were waiting for him.

As always Karl Humboldt was leading. He pushed himself away from the hitching-rail outside the courthouse and with his younger brothers flanking him followed Lincoln across the road to the sheriff's office.

'Suppose you're pinning the sheriff's death on him as well as Wesley's,' he said, his tone belligerent.

Lincoln stomped to a halt in the road. 'Now why would *you* think that?'

'I know how you lawmen work. You drag in the nearest man to the body then pin his name on to all the crimes you ain't got a face for.'

'I haven't pinned any murder on Alex ... yet. Murphy has set his trial for Wednesday and he'll get himself a fair hearing.' Lincoln flashed a smile. 'So if you know anything that'll help, don't keep it to yourself.'

Karl snorted his breath through his nostrils, then paced round to stand before Lincoln.

'I won't ever help no lawman.'

'Then help yourself.' Lincoln raised his eyebrows. 'Before he died Wesley told me you weren't in the Golden Star saloon on the night Ben died.'

'I can find plenty of live witnesses who saw me in the saloon that night,' Karl said, looking around confidently as if he could produce those people with a click of the fingers.

'I'm sure you can *persuade* plenty of people to come forward, and that's why I've not arrested you. I'm giving you enough space to make a mistake, then your brother won't be the only one facing a trial.'

Karl cast a meaningful glance at the sheriff's office, then at his brothers.

'We'll make sure Alex don't face no trial.'

'If that means what I reckon it means,' Lincoln snapped, placing his hands on his hips, 'I'll be coming for you before you get that chance to make a mistake.'

Over Karl's shoulder Lincoln saw Deputy Curtis slowly open the door. Curtis had a rifle held low and dangling, but he held it in a manner that was still menacing enough to make Wilhelm and Heinrich flinch. Karl glanced back to see what had worried them, then slumped his shoulders a mite as some of the fight went out of him. Karl still fixed Lincoln with a firm gaze for a moment, then turned on his heel.

'Later,' he said. Then with slow arrogance he and his brothers loped off down the boardwalk.

Lincoln watched the brothers leave, then followed Curtis into the office.

'They've been out there for the last hour,' Curtis said, gulping, 'goading each other on to say something.'

'Surprised they got themselves the courage to almost say something this time.'

'Oh they will, they will.' Curtis lowered his voice. 'Did the judge believe Alex's story?'

'He'd like to, but right now Alex is our only suspect.' Lincoln swung round to consider Alex, now sitting in the same cell as he'd occupied the day before. He raised his voice so that the prisoner could hear him. 'He'll have to give me more before the judge will believe him.'

Lincoln had hoped that after he'd been to see the judge he'd see some sign that Alex was prepared to talk openly, but Alex still had the same hunched posture and firm-set jaw as earlier. With a steady and heavy tread to command Alex's attention, Lincoln headed across the office and looked through the bars at him.

'I've told you everything,' Alex said, staring at the floor. 'I followed this man. He disappeared.'

'And how did you get the blood on your clothes?'

'My brothers gave me a whupping,' Alex whined. He looked up and met Lincoln's eye for the first time. 'I can show you the bruises.'

Alex did have several bruises on his hands and face, but Lincoln still shook his head.

'Was that a whupping for setting fire to the saloon, or for getting caught?' Lincoln waited for a reply that didn't come, then continued. 'Put an end to this, Alex. Either admit you did it or give me the name of this man with a face like a skull.'

'I don't know no name.'

'That attitude will get you a stretched neck some day soon. If you're hoping Karl will break you out of there before that day comes, I don't reckon he's got the nerve to do it.'

Alex gulped. His hands began to shake.

'He wouldn't try to break me out, would he?'

Lincoln noted Alex's response and it helped to firm up the gut-reaction he'd had ever since he'd heard of Karl Humboldt. He gestured for Deputy Curtis to throw him the keys to the cell, then opened the door and went inside. Two cots were in the cell. Lincoln sat on the one opposite to Alex and considered him with his hands resting on his knees. When he spoke, he lowered his voice, hoping that speaking to him close to and without the bars between them might help Alex to accept what he said.

'Despite the evidence against you, I don't reckon you're the kind of man who'd kill. But twice you've been the only person close to a serious crime, and both times you acted suspiciously.' Lincoln raised his eyebrows for emphasis. 'So tell me what you were really doing and prove to me that you're innocent.'

'I can't.'

Lincoln hadn't expected Alex to provide an answer just yet, but he noted Alex's choice of words. He hadn't said that he didn't know what had happened; he just couldn't talk about it. Lincoln leaned forward. The cell door obligingly creaked open a few inches, offering its own inducement.

'To my mind the only reason a man might risk getting the noose is that he's even more scared of something else happening than he is of death. As you won't speak, I'll tell you what I reckon happened. Someone killed Sheriff Ben Pringle to settle an old grudge, then told Wesley Jameson to give him an alibi. You and that someone threatened to burn down his saloon if he didn't comply. You didn't intend to carry out your threat, but you accidentally dropped the lamp and the fire started anyhow.'

'It wasn't like that,' Alex murmured, his downcast eyes and low tone suggesting Lincoln was close to the truth.

'You both panicked and ran, but when the flames got out of hand you had a change of heart and went back for Wesley. But the flames beat you back and so you tried to dispose of the evidence. After I arrested you, you covered up for your accomplice because he was someone close to you – your brother Karl.'

Alex gulped and darted his gaze around the cell, his shock implying Lincoln's assumption was correct.

'It wasn't Karl who did it,' he murmured.

Lincoln again noted Alex's choice of words. He couldn't tell him who had killed Ben and Wesley, and it wasn't Karl who did it either, but neither was it Alex himself But one thing was sure – he was protecting someone.

'Tell me the truth, Alex,' Lincoln said, lowering his voice. 'A man can take ten minutes to die dangling on the end of a rope and nothing can be worse than an end like that. It's your choice, the truth or the noose.'

Alex didn't reply for a full minute. When he did speak he looked at the floor between his feet and his voice was gruff and faded to a whisper several times.

'The truth is I did set fire to the saloon. This man paid me ten dollars to throw an oil-lamp through the back door. I didn't think it'd burn the saloon down though and I did go back to try to get Wesley out. But I sure didn't kill him and I don't know nothing about Sheriff Pringle.'

'I'd like to believe you, Alex, but you'll have to give me more than that. Who was this man?'

'He didn't give me no name. He kept in the shadows.' He looked up and met Lincoln's eyes. 'It was like I said, Marshal, he had a face like a skull, all cold and white. I saw him again this morning and I followed him, but I couldn't catch up with him.'

'Why did you follow him? Because I don't believe you were aiming to be a good citizen.'

Alex gulped and gave a shame-faced grin.

'I wanted to get more money off him in return for not talking to you.'

This had the ring of truth, making Lincoln smile.

'When he paid you he must have said something that'll help me find him. If you think of what that is, tell me.'

Lincoln fixed Alex with his firm gaze then rocked forward, preparing to leave him to mull over his words, but Alex coughed, halting him.

'He did mention a name when he paid me the money. I don't reckon it was his own name but someone else in his pay.'

'And the name?'

Alex closed his eyes and under his breath he whispered a name. Lincoln considered Alex's answer. He judged it as being just expected enough to be a lie, but just bizarre enough to be the truth.

'You've done the right thing, son,' Lincoln said, placing a hand on Alex's shoulder before he left the cell.

Deputy Curtis was watching him, clearly not having heard Alex's response, but Lincoln didn't feel minded to reveal what he'd said.

'Curtis,' he said, 'I'm leaving town. I'll be back tomorrow if I get lucky. Longer if I don't.'

'Do what you want,' Curtis said, shrugging, as they walked to the door. 'You ain't my boss.'

'While I'm gone keep probing Alex's story and keep those brothers under watch.' Lincoln stopped and glared at Curtis. 'But most important – work on that attitude of yours.'

'What attitude?' Curtis snapped, slapping his hands on his hips and leaning forward to glare back at Lincoln.

Lincoln ground his hands into tight fists to keep his rising temper under control and merely returned Curtis's annoyed gaze.

'It's like this – when I get back I'll be closer to finding the man who killed Ben and I'll need the help of someone with dedication, not someone who just wants to argue with me.' Lincoln let the rest of his threat remain unsaid, trusting that Curtis would understand he could always find another deputy, and sure enough Curtis sneered.

'I'm a deputy sheriff in a town that ain't got no sheriff. I'm not a deputy marshal. You can't do nothing to me.'

'I can't,' Lincoln said, 'but you've had a problem with me since the moment I arrived. So just tell it to me straight. Why?'

Curtis hitched up his belt while glancing around, his furtive eyes showing he was debating whether to speak his mind, then shrugged.

'All right. The sheriff ain't here no more and I want to be the next sheriff. I had a chance except you being here makes me look bad.'

This revelation didn't surprise Lincoln.

'You look bad because you are bad. If you had found Ben's killer, Mayor Ellison wouldn't have called me in.' Lincoln was minded to continue berating Curtis, but he decided to have one last attempt at offering him encouragement. 'But it doesn't have to be that way. When I find the killer, it'll look good for you too, and it'll teach you something about being a lawman. Think about that while I'm gone instead of looking for reasons to argue with me.'

Curtis bunched his jaw, his wild eyes reflecting his angry thoughts before he got his temper under control with a firm slap of a fist against his thigh.

'Any other orders, boss?' he grunted.

Lincoln ignored the contempt in Curtis's tone.

'Tell Judge Murphy I'm following a lead on the murders and make sure he doesn't start Alex's trial until I get back.'

'Don't worry,' Curtis said, delivering a forced smile. 'You can trust me.'

With sundown an hour away, Lincoln rode into Carter's Creek, a run-down cow-town along the trail which, without the benefit of a railroad, was now not faring as well as Independence was.

Jack Porter, the gambler who had won $25,000 off Billy Stone, had ridden out of town after he'd collected his money. As Black Point, the next nearest town, was a day away, Lincoln reckoned that Jack had to have headed here.

So firstly he looked over the batwings of the town's only saloon and sure enough Jack was playing poker with three cowboys at the back of the saloon. The other players were rough-clad and wouldn't provide Jack with the sort of return he'd gained last night, but Lincoln reckoned that gamblers like Jack practised their skills at every opportunity.

Lincoln nudged through the batwings, then weaved through the tables until he stood behind Jack.

One of the cowboys looked up at Lincoln, but his gaze caught on Lincoln's star and he drew the brim of his hat down.

Jack followed the cowboy's gaze and glanced over his shoulder. A huge smile spread.

'Howdy, Marshal Lincoln Hawk,' he said, his voice loud and contented. 'Do you want to play real poker with me again? Stakes ain't as good as they were last night, but we're all having a mighty fine time.'

'Nope. I just want to ask you some questions.'

'Not yet.' Jack glanced around the table, smiling, then leaned to his side and placed a hand beside his mouth. 'You'll have to wait until I get dealt some worse cards than these. My luck just ain't changing today.'

The cowboy opposite Jack snorted and threw his cards down while Lincoln raised his eyebrows then leaned down to place his mouth beside Jack's ear.

'Now, at the bar,' he said, keeping his voice loud enough for the other players to hear. Then he lowered his voice to a whisper. 'I know what you did.'

Lincoln stood back and exchanged long stares with Jack. As the cowboys muttered amongst themselves, Jack threw his cards on the table.

'If you'll excuse me, gentlemen,' he said, delivering a short bow, all sign of his former jovial mood gone. 'Perhaps my cards aren't as hot as I claimed, and I have some business with the lawman.'

Jack smoothed his jacket then stood and headed to the bar. Lincoln joined him and tapped his foot on the rail as Jack ordered two whiskeys. When they arrived, Jack hunched over his drink and stared deep into the whiskey. He swirled the liquor, then placed the glass down without drinking.

'All right, Marshal,' he said, his voice low. 'What do you reckon you know?'

Lincoln matched Jack's posture as he hunched over his whiskey.

'It's like this – a gambler takes Billy Stone for twenty-five thousand dollars in front of a lawman, a judge and the town mayor. A man who can do that is either mighty skilled, mighty lucky, or was just doing something so brazen that nobody spotted what it was.' Lincoln sipped his whiskey. 'Until afterwards when we all got to talking and comparing notes about what we'd seen.'

Jack frowned. 'You got proof? Because you can't go accusing people like that.'

'I don't need no proof.' Lincoln gulped his whiskey and slammed the empty glass beside Jack's full glass. 'Because until five seconds ago, I didn't know I needed to prove anything.'

Jack swirled round to face Lincoln, his eyes blazing, but as Lincoln met his gaze, a smile invaded the corners of his mouth.

'Well played, Marshal. With that level voice and stone gaze, you'll make a fine poker-player one day.'

'I like to gamble, but you're wrong. I'm just too fair-minded.'

'Perhaps you are and that forces me to tell you that you called my bluff too early.' Jack raised his whiskey and took a long gulp. 'So unless you've got proof I cheated Billy, I'd be obliged if you'd leave me to finish my game.'

Jack gulped back the last of his whiskey and tipped his hat then turned to walk past Lincoln. Lincoln grabbed his arm, halting him.

'Trouble is, I'm not investigating Billy's losses at the poker-table. I'm investigating the death of Sheriff Ben Pringle and now

Wesley Jameson. And I reckon I have enough on you already to take you back to Independence to face trial.'

Jack blinked hard, his mouth falling open and his eyes opening wide in what, if Lincoln didn't know what a consummate poker-player Jack was, would have been a convincing representation of utter shock.

'I've never met either man and I didn't even know Wesley was dead.'

With a snap of his wrist, Lincoln released Jack's arm.

'Then you'll have nothing to fear from me. Be open with me and I won't take you back to Independence and throw you in a cell.'

Jack tipped back his hat. 'All right. When did Wesley Jameson die?'

'This morning.' Lincoln smiled. 'And you left town this morning.'

'I did, but it was before Wesley died.'

'And how do you know *when* exactly this morning Wesley died?'

Jack glanced away. 'The town was quiet when I left, and I heard no gunshots.'

'I never said that Wesley had been shot.' Lincoln raised his eyebrows. 'Your attempts at being open ain't convincing me that you're innocent.'

Jack tapped a knuckle on the bar with an

irritated rhythm.

'I was surmising and you aren't tricking me into revealing anything because I have nothing to reveal,' he said, snapping out the words. 'Besides, the train passed through Independence this morning. When I left town a whole mess of people were heading for the station and one of them must have seen me leave.'

'I'm sure a man with twenty-five thousand dollars to his name can find plenty of friendly witnesses.'

Jack accepted Lincoln's sarcasm with barely a flicker to his level gaze.

'Quit the snide comments and just tell me why you reckon I'm responsible and I'll explain why you're wrong.'

When Lincoln didn't answer immediately Jack smiled, then beckoned the bartender over. He ordered another two whiskeys, his voice regaining its earlier calm tone.

Lincoln leaned on the bar until the bartender had poured the drinks, then turned to Jack.

'Some people have waited years for an opening in Independence's monthly poker-game, and yet you get to play at the first opportunity. And gamblers who bet five thousand dollars on a single hand of poker don't ride into Independence too often, but such a man just happens to be available on the night that Wesley Jameson ain't available.'

'That was my luck.'

Lincoln took a steady sip of his drink, then placed it on the bar before him. He fingered the glass, pushing it round in a circle, then turned to Jack.

'Perhaps it was, but the man whose place you took got himself a whole heap of bad luck, as did the man whose place I took.'

Jack swirled his whiskey then sipped it, his shoulders hunching.

'If that's the best you can do, I'll just have to come with you and answer your allegations.' Jack gave a resigned smile. 'It won't be hard.'

Lincoln spread his hands. 'Then we'll be going just as soon as–'

Lincoln flinched back as Jack's hand swirled round, the movement sudden and swift, but Jack was only clutching the whiskey glass. The whiskey spouted from the glass and splashed into Lincoln's face, burning into his eyes. Lincoln backed away for a pace, batting his face and shaking his head to regain his vision before Jack could act again. But footfalls pattered past him as

Jack ran for the door.

With his eyes still watering and his vision blurred, Lincoln headed after him. He saw Jack run past the saloon window and disappear from view. Then he pushed through the swinging batwings and held on to them as he shook the last of the whiskey from his eyes.

Jack had already disappeared from view and the few people out on the road were all going about their business serenely.

Lincoln hurried past the window and down the boardwalk. Jack had had only a few seconds on him and he hadn't had enough time to cross the road or reach the nearest alley, a hundred yards down the road. He must have slipped through the door in one of the next two buildings, the hotel or the church.

Lincoln also noted that Jack's horse was still standing outside the mercantile across the road, adding further weight to the possibility that he hadn't had enough time to leave town. So he took a pace backwards to place his back to the saloon wall. For the next few minutes Lincoln waited for Jack to make a run for his horse.

Jack didn't appear and so slowly Lincoln had to accept that a man with $25,000 on him might not feel a need to return to his horse. As the hotel was the nearest building, he headed there first.

A smiling man behind the reception desk greeted him. Even before Lincoln had completed his question as to whether he'd seen Jack, the man reported he hadn't seen anyone enter his hotel all day, all the time nodding and smiling with an almost desperate desire to please. His response was just a little too quick and enthusiastic, but Lincoln still thanked him politely for his help in a loud voice, feigning that he believed him, and left the hotel. He slipped into the church doorway and waited.

Several minutes passed before Lincoln's hunch paid off and he saw Jack look out of the hotel door and dart his gaze around. Then Jack rolled his shoulders and paced out on to the boardwalk and across the road, heading briskly for his horse.

Lincoln let him get half-way across the road, then followed, placing his feet to the ground carefully, but the moment Lincoln left the boardwalk, the alert Jack flinched, turned on his heel and saw him. He broke into a run, as did Lincoln.

Jack pounded across the ground, ignoring his own horse and heading for the nearest available mount.

On the run, Jack reached the hitching-rail then unlooped the reins. He moved to swing himself up on to the horse, but was too slow and couldn't avoid Lincoln slamming into him. Lincoln grabbed his hips and tugged while Jack kicked out. His foot whistled through the air and missed Lincoln, the action letting Lincoln get a firm grip of his leg and bodily yank him off the horse. Jack squirmed as he fell, managing to unbalance Lincoln and the two men fell to the ground, entangled.

Jack fought his way to his knees then clawed himself to his feet, knocking Lincoln on his back in the process, but Lincoln braced his back against the ground and kicked Jack's feet from him. Jack went down, landing heavily on his chest. He lay winded, then slowly rolled over and by the time he looked up, Lincoln was standing over him with his gun drawn and aimed down at his chest. Lincoln shook his head.

'Seems as if you're coming with me,' he said, 'after all.'

CHAPTER 6

'You wasted your time arresting me,' Jack Porter said, glaring at Lincoln while clutching the reins with his bound hands. 'I didn't kill Wesley Jameson or Sheriff Pringle.'

While Lincoln had been making ready to move out of town, Jack had repeatedly protested his innocence. Lincoln had ignored his pleas but now that he had Jack bound and secured to his horse as they headed back to Independence, Lincoln decided to respond.

'Then why run?' he said.

'I play poker for money and I took plenty off Billy Stone last night. I just wanted to keep my money.'

Lincoln didn't speak for a while, letting his silence prey on Jack's mind.

'You have one chance to convince me you're not involved,' he said eventually, his voice low. He drew his horse to a halt and smiled. 'Tell me who hired you to get into the poker-game.'

Jack snorted. 'I've never needed no encouragement to get into a poker-game.'

'Perhaps not, but I reckon someone hired you to come to Independence and play poker with Billy Stone on the day the Golden Star saloon burnt down, the only time there'd be a spare place at the table.'

'You got that wrong. I arrived in town a week ago.'

Lincoln chuckled. 'A week! Now that sure is interesting. Ben Pringle died a week ago.'

Jack sighed as he turned away from Lincoln's firm gaze. Long moments passed in silence.

'All right, if someone did hire me,' he murmured, his tone sounding defeated, 'will you let me go?'

'Nope. You'll just get my gratitude, and a man who's facing a term in prison could do with a lawman for a friend.'

'Then can I keep the money I won?'

'I can't promise you that either, but I can promise you that if you don't give me a name, you'll face charges that are one hell of a lot more serious than cheating at poker.'

Jack stared straight ahead, rocking his head from side to side, then turned to look at him.

'I can't give you a name.'

'Then a description.'

'I can't give you that either. I didn't see his face. He was in the shadows. I reckon he was wearing a mask to disguise himself.'

'And he hired you to kill Ben Pringle and Wesley Jameson?'

'Hey,' Jack said, waving his bound hands. 'He just hired me to get in that poker-game. You've got no reason to think I was behind their deaths. If that's the way you're conducting this investigation, I'm not telling you nothing else.'

Jack jutted his chin with a mixture of mock indignation and possibly genuine annoyance. As promised, he ignored Lincoln's subsequent questions and so Lincoln relented from his questioning and hurried his horse on.

He now faced the problem of getting his prisoner back to town. As he wouldn't be able to get back to Independence during daylight hours, Lincoln looked for a good place to stop for the night. Ultimately, he chose a spot beside the river.

Lincoln acted cautiously, never letting Jack out of his sight, but as it turned out, Jack gave him no trouble. Despite the gambler's quick reactions and quick mind, he didn't make the break for freedom that

Lincoln had expected him to try, or even looked as if he were waiting for a chance to run. This suggested he was either innocent or was cool enough to have convinced himself that Lincoln wouldn't be able to prove his guilt.

With Lincoln aiming to reach town quickly the next day they set off early. A night's sleep along with, presumably, some sombre reflection, had encouraged Jack to be in a more talkative frame of mind and so as they rode along Lincoln questioned him. He varied his method of probing so he could compare the answers he received and seek out discrepancies. Jack was cautious with his replies, but from the little he did reveal, and from the clues Lincoln had picked up previously, Lincoln pieced together some of what had been happening.

Someone linked to, or perhaps in, the photograph that depicted several of Independence's key people had decided to take revenge on the others in that photograph, presumably to settle an old score. Alex's and Jack's description of the man, along with Lincoln's brief sighting, suggested that this man lived in Independence and wore a mask that looked like a skull to hide his identity.

For several months this man had terrorized Sheriff Ben Pringle before he either killed him or hired someone – perhaps Karl Humboldt or Jack Porter – to kill him. Then he'd moved on to Wesley Jameson. He'd hired Alex to burn down Wesley's saloon and hired Jack Porter to start work on his next target by bankrupting Billy Stone in a poker game. Then the masked man, or his hired hand, had shot Wesley. On balance, Lincoln reckoned Jack or Karl were the more likely culprits as he was getting the feeling that the masked man was someone who hired others to settle his scores.

The sun was at its highest when they rode back into Independence and by then Lincoln had resolved to stop giving Karl enough leeway to make a fatal mistake and just throw him in a cell alongside Alex and Jack. Then he'd keep probing at all three men's stories until he uncovered the full truth. He was sure one of them would snap after they'd festered away in a cell for a few days with the thought preying on their minds that they might pay the price for someone else's vendetta.

The first thing Lincoln noticed as he approached the sheriff's office was that few people were about. The second was that

Karl Humboldt wasn't lurking outside. He hadn't expected the Humboldt brothers to give up on their vigil so quickly and so he was already on alert for something to be wrong when he dismounted. He led Jack inside and immediately noticed that all the cells were empty.

Deputy Curtis was standing before his desk and talking in low tones with Judge Murphy who was sitting with his feet on the desk. When the door creaked open both men fell silent and looked at him. Then with a grunt of acknowledgement to Lincoln, Murphy rocked his feet down to the floor and stood.

'What you bring him back for?' he asked, nodding at Lincoln's prisoner.

'Jack Porter was the man I went to find.' Lincoln looked at Curtis. 'Where's Alex?'

Curtis flashed a faint smile, which to Lincoln's eyes looked like a self-satisfied smirk.

'He ain't here no more,' Curtis said. 'We had his trial this morning.'

'This morning! I told you to...' Lincoln sighed. 'Well, I'm just going to have to drag him and his no-good brother back in.'

Lincoln shoved Jack towards the cells, then collected a key.

'You won't be doing no more questioning of Alex Humboldt,' Curtis said, following him.

'I know his brothers will reckon I'm hassling him after he was released for the second time in two days.' Lincoln placed Jack in a cell then locked it. 'But I can't worry about that.'

He turned to see that Curtis was smiling, his lively eyes drinking in Lincoln's stern expression in an eager way that sent a tremor of concern rippling through Lincoln's mind.

'You don't understand,' Curtis said with obvious relish. 'You can't question Alex no more because...'

Curtis delivered a self-satisfied cackle, the act making him cough and giving Murphy the opportunity to speak up.

'What Deputy Curtis is trying to say,' Murphy said, 'is that I didn't find Alex innocent. I found him guilty of killing Wesley Jameson and Ben Pringle.' Murphy gave a sorry shrug. 'We hanged him this morning.'

Lincoln swayed, his shock making him lightheaded and nauseated. He couldn't say with any assurance yet that Alex hadn't killed Wesley, but he reckoned the other culprits he had in mind were more likely killers than Alex Humboldt.

'Why did you go ahead with the trial?' Lincoln demanded, swinging round to confront Judge Murphy. 'I told you to wait until I returned.'

The judge looked at Curtis, who was biting his lip to avoid smiling too much, then beckoned for Lincoln to follow him outside. Out on the boardwalk he looked up and down the road, confirming that nobody was nearby before he replied.

'You never told me to delay the trial.'

'I told Curtis to give you the message.'

'I didn't get that message.'

Lincoln winced. Curtis was incompetent, but this failing was extreme even for him.

'Then what in tarnation was the reasoning behind that decision?'

'I don't have to explain my decisions.'

'You don't, but I sure as hell would appreciate one when I'm sure you've hanged the wrong man.'

'I convicted based on the evidence and your statement, and they were damning.'

'There was no evidence, or at least nothing that Alex couldn't explain away.'

'Except for one thing. Deputy Curtis searched Alex more thoroughly. He found another copy of the photograph Wesley brought out the fire. It had Ben's name on the back. Alex wouldn't explain how he got it and so I concluded he took it off Ben when he killed him. With him admitting to burning down Walter's saloon, I also concluded he killed Walter.'

Lincoln conceded that this interpretation of events could be correct with a curt nod.

'Show me the photograph.'

'There's no need, not now the matter is closed.'

'The matter ain't closed. Despite your reasoning, I'm not entirely convinced you found the right man guilty. I have Jack Porter in a cell, and I need to question him about Wesley's and Ben's deaths. That picture might tell me who's really behind this.'

Murphy glanced away to look across the road at the courthouse. He tapped a foot on the boardwalk, perhaps as he considered then dismissed the shameful thought that he might have convicted the wrong man. He got himself under control with a rolling of the shoulders.

'It's now irrelevant. Alex has been hanged for the crimes and the matter ends there. You will release Jack Porter immediately, and you will stop harassing Karl Humboldt.'

Lincoln opened his mouth, aiming to continue arguing his case, but then closed it. Murphy had acted with atypical haste in dealing with Alex, and Lincoln was getting the feeling that other members of the poker-group would be in the photograph, and so would be involved in whatever was happening here. If that were the case, one of those men would be Murphy. It was unthinkable that the judge was covering up for his own actions, but then again the members of the poker-group were tightly knit. It was possible he had acted rashly in a misguided attempt to help a friend.

Whatever the reasoning, Lincoln reckoned that arguing any further would be pointless.

'All right,' he said. 'Now that Alex Humboldt is dead Jack Porter goes free.'

CHAPTER 7

Lincoln held the cell door open for Jack Porter to leave.

'Now,' Jack said, grinning as he stood, 'that must be shortest visit to a cell I've ever had.'

'And I'll make sure,' Lincoln said, 'it'll be a short time before you're back in there.'

'You can't arrest me. Your deputy has been so good as to explain the situation to me and–'

'Quit gloating and get out.' Lincoln waited while Jack collected his hat and took his time in walking to the door before he spoke up again. 'But don't leave town, I'll be talking to you later.'

'I'll look forward to it,' Jack said, giving a mocking smile. Then he tipped his hat to Lincoln and left, leaving Lincoln alone with Curtis.

Lincoln took deep breaths to calm himself before he paced over to Curtis's desk and faced him.

'The last thing I said to you before I went

after Jack was to make sure the trial didn't go ahead,' he said, just managing to keep his voice calm and his temper under control. 'But Judge Murphy brought it forward. So what did you say to him?'

Curtis shrugged, then leaned back in his chair and placed his hands behind his head.

'Not much. But as you didn't tell me nothing about why you were–'

'Stop your whining! You made a big mistake and an innocent man is dead because of it.'

'Odd that. Sheriff Pringle always told me we don't decide who's guilty and who's innocent, we just bring 'em in. Well, Judge Murphy looked at the evidence and he decided. So don't blame me.'

Lincoln had to concede this was right, but it didn't change the fact that Curtis had failed him just once too often. He folded his arms and ground his teeth as he forced himself to keep his anger at bay while he learned everything he could about the situation.

'How come you only found this evidence after I'd gone?' he asked.

'I was only looking for weapons, and a photograph ain't a weapon.'

Lincoln conceded this point with a slow nod, then leaned forward, eager despite his anger to hear the answer to his next question.

'And what did the picture show?'

'You'd seen half of it already. It had Sheriff Pringle, Wesley Jameson and Sheckley Dolby–'

'Who's he?'

'Never met him, but he used to work for the judge a few years back. He was a good man from what I've heard.'

'Obliged for identifying him,' Lincoln said, noting that the judge had claimed he didn't recognize this person when they were playing poker two nights ago. 'What was on the other half?'

Curtis raised his eyebrows then tipped back his hat. He delivered a whooping whistle.

'Now there was something to behold. It had four more men standing before this hanging man. It sure was a terrible sight, him all dangling there with these men posing right in front of the body.'

'Did you recognize the hanging man?'

'Nope, but then again his face was all distorted. It's hard to describe what he looked like. His face looked like...' Curtis waved his hands as he searched for the right words. 'It looked like a skull.'

Lincoln avoided reacting to this piece of information.

'And the other four men?'

'There was Lenox Devere...' Curtis paused, presumably because Doc Thoreau had told him that he was the man they'd fished out of the river. Again Lincoln avoided reacting. In a curious way he was even pleased to hear this revelation.

'And the other men?'

'Billy Stone, Mayor Ellison and Judge Murphy.'

Although Lincoln had expected to hear those names, he couldn't help but react this time and he delivered an irritated snort.

'All the old poker-group except Doc Thoreau.'

'Thoreau only joined a few years ago.'

'And Sheckley Dolby and Lenox Devere?'

'Sheckley used to play, but I doubt the likes of Lenox Devere would be welcome in that group.'

Lincoln nodded, noting that despite his faults, Curtis could provide useful information sometimes. In some ways what he'd told him had helped to clarify the judge's and the mayor's actions in pretending they didn't remember the photograph. Maybe they didn't want to be reminded of an event from their past of which they weren't proud. On the other hand that event had led to fatal consequences for three of the people in the photograph, and Lincoln didn't reckon the matter would end there.

Lincoln resisted the temptation to lecture Curtis about his failings again and after forcing himself to thank him for the information he left the sheriff's office. He headed down the road to the Rising Sun saloon and wasn't surprised when his guess proved to be correct. Jack Porter was leaning on the bar.

'Now,' Jack said, eyeing the advancing Lincoln, 'there was me thinking you'd let me enjoy one drink in peace before you came looking for me.'

Lincoln leaned on the bar beside Jack. 'You'll never get to enjoy any peace until I prove you're a killer.'

'But I'm not. Alex Humboldt killed Sheriff Pringle and Wesley Jameson. Everyone says so.'

'I reckon there's plenty more to what happened there than what's come out so far, and I'll prove you were involved.'

'You won't get far. Now that someone's swung today for the crimes you want to heap on me, I reckon it won't be long before people are calling me the new man they couldn't hang.'

'New?'

Jack shrugged. 'You're full of questions, but I don't need to answer any of them because you can't touch me.'

'That confidence is misplaced.' Lincoln gave a harsh smile. 'So watch out. Soon I'll come looking for you.'

'You can do that.' Jack glanced over Lincoln's shoulder, 'but if I were you, I'd worry more about those who've already come looking for you.'

Lincoln followed the direction of Jack's gaze to see that the encounter he'd dreaded was already upon him. Karl Humboldt and his two brothers were pushing through the batwings.

Lincoln watched the three surly brothers approach, his feelings on them being mixed. He was sure these notorious troublemakers were involved in the crimes Judge Murphy had forbade him from investigating, but after what had happened to their younger brother, Lincoln could understand their need to lash out at someone.

'Just got back in town,' he said, when Karl stomped to a halt before him. 'I've only just heard the news.'

'So,' Karl muttered, 'you couldn't even be bothered to be here for his trial.'

Again Lincoln was torn, sympathizing with him for how his actions would appear, while not wanting to tell the truth and so sounding as though he was criticizing Judge Murphy.

'I tried to get back in time, but I was unavoidably detained.' Lincoln pushed himself away from the bar and moved to walk by the brothers. 'I'm sorry it had to end this way.'

Karl stepped to the side to block Lincoln's way, his brothers moving to flank him and make sure Lincoln couldn't reach the door.

'You claim you're sorry,' he muttered with contempt as around him the customers watched the developing confrontation with interest. 'But I don't believe you.'

'Then don't. I'm leaving,' Lincoln said, deliberately not meeting Karl's eye. 'Move out of my way.'

'Or you'll kill us, is that it? Like you killed our younger brother just because he was in your way.'

'It wasn't like that. Judge Murphy heard all the evidence and decided against him. My opinion on the matter is irrelevant.'

Despite his contempt for Karl, Lincoln hoped he might pick up his veiled criticism of the decision, the furthest he could go without being disloyal, but Karl was too angry to interpret such subtle comments.

'We all know what you thought about Alex,' he said standing up to Lincoln and jabbing a firm finger at his chest. 'You ordered the judge to get him dealt with as quickly as he could and you didn't have the stomach to stay around for the hanging. It all stinks.'

Lincoln had to agree with that but he shook his head.

'I can't order Judge Murphy to do anything.' He looked down at the finger until Karl removed it, then looked him in the eye. 'Now stand aside before you say something you'll regret.'

Karl licked his lips, suggesting everything was going according to his plan of forcing Lincoln into a confrontation.

'I'm staying here until I've said it all – unless you reckon you can make me be quiet.'

Lincoln spread his hands. 'I've got nothing to hide. Speak your mind.'

Karl took a deep breath, his lively grin showing how much he relished giving Lincoln his answer.

'Deputy Curtis says you've got plenty to hide. You ordered him to get the trial over and done with before you got back. He didn't want to do it, but he had his orders, and with your evidence, the judge found him guilty.'

Lincoln was speechless for several seconds before he could blurt out a response.

'Curtis told you this?'

'Sure did.' Karl snorted a laugh, seemingly pleased to have got a reaction out of Lincoln. 'He told me the full story. And I'll make sure the whole town knows what you did.'

Lincoln was minded to ignore Karl's version of events, but sadly this statement had the ring of truth. Curtis had behaved shiftily rather than with his usual sloth since his return and there had to be a reason for that.

'Then tell the town the truth,' Lincoln said, raising his voice so everyone could hear, 'I never gave Curtis that order. I told him to wait until I got back before ... before taking Alex to trial.'

Karl snorted, his sneer probably showing that he took Lincoln's hesitant delivery as a sign of guilt and not of his trying to find the right words that'd avoid him criticizing the judge.

'I don't believe you and neither will anyone else.'

Lincoln reckoned there was nothing more to be gained by trying to prove his innocence right now, when faced by Karl's anger, and he took a long pace to stand toe to toe with him.

'Move,' he said.

For several seconds Karl met his gaze until with a mocking sneer on his face and an over-exaggerated movement of his legs that added to the mockery he paced to the side. He waited until Lincoln had walked between his two brothers before he spoke again.

'I've moved, but next time...'

Lincoln stopped, listening to the two other brothers mutter threats under their breaths, then he set off. As he headed outside, he heard several customers speak up and demand to know the full story from the brothers, but Lincoln resisted the temptation to go back in and shout down their lies.

Right now he wanted to hear the full story for himself.

With a firm gait he stormed down the road to the sheriff's office, then kicked open the door.

'Curtis,' he shouted in a voice that echoed throughout the law office, 'get up!'

Curtis looked up from under his hat. He delivered an unnecessarily long yawn then stretched and slowly got off his chair.

'What's wrong?'

'I've just met Karl Humboldt.'

Curtis shrugged, his downcast eyes registering shame and when he spoke his tone was guarded.

'I guess he wasn't too happy.'

'You guessed right, and the reason he's so angry is he's got it into his head that Alex is dead because of me.'

'Oh?' Curtis said cautiously.

'Based on your pathetic behaviour. So far I have been prepared to accept that you were stupid enough to not tell Murphy to hold off on the trial, but what I've just heard is something else. You told Karl I ordered you to close the investigation and get Alex hanged as soon as possible.'

Curtis gulped. 'I was just talking. You can't blame me for that.'

'I can when everybody believes him.'

Lincoln backed away to the door, dragged it open, then pointed outside.

'What do you want me to do?' Curtis asked.

'I'm giving you a choice. Either go to the saloon and tell everybody what really happened, or have me kick you outside, then all the way down the road until you tell everybody what really happened.'

'I don't have to take that from you.'

'You do if you want to work as a lawman in this town again. Now get out there and start talking.'

With as much dignity as he could muster Curtis walked past Lincoln and headed outside, but he stopped on the boardwalk and while looking into the road spoke up.

'You can't speak to me like that. I don't work for you.'

'Accepted.' Lincoln backed away a pace then delivered a swinging kick to Curtis's rump that sent him sprawling to his knees on the boardwalk. 'Now get talking.'

Curtis shuffled round to face Lincoln, then got to his feet and waggled a finger at Lincoln, his face reddening.

'I'll sure tell everyone the truth about you, don't you worry. I'll–'

Curtis didn't get to finish his threat as Lincoln paced up to him and shoved him off the boardwalk. Curtis stumbled, half-turning as he thrust out a leg to stop himself falling and so letting Lincoln deliver another huge kick to his rump that sent him ploughing head first into the dirt.

Lincoln stood over him. 'How far down the road do you want me to kick you, Curtis, before you start talking sense?'

Curtis lay on his chest spitting dirt, then slowly got to his feet and faced up to Lincoln.

'Then do it. Show everyone in town I was right about you.'

'Obliged for the offer.' Lincoln rolled his shoulders then drew back his foot ready to kick Curtis again. 'Everyone knows I don't like no-good liars.'

Curtis stood his ground and Lincoln thought he'd was going to let him kick him again but at the last moment Curtis panicked. He gulped, then turned on his heel and scampered away. Lincoln hurried after him and managed to deliver another glancing kick at his fleeing form before Curtis hightailed it away from him.

Lincoln noted several people were out and watching the altercation, so for their benefit he shouted after him.

'You're a liar, Curtis!'

Lincoln watched him, noting that he did head into the saloon, then returned to the law office, but found that he still had one interested observer – Mayor Ellison. He was standing beside the door and shaking his head.

'Two lawmen fighting in the road looks bad, Lincoln,' he said.

Lincoln beckoned for the mayor to follow

him inside.

'That was one lawman and one no-good varmint. But I had no choice. Curtis has been telling everyone it's my fault about what happened to Alex.'

Ellison provided a comforting wince, his guarded reaction implying this wasn't news to him.

'Unfortunate incident all round, but I'll reiterate Murphy's advice. Just move on and forget about Jack Porter.'

'I will, but what happened to Ben and Wesley is linked and–'

'I know what you're trying to say, but that doesn't excuse you starting a vendetta of your own against Jack Porter or Karl Humboldt or now Deputy Curtis.'

'Curtis lied, and I'll make sure everyone knows that.'

Ellison sighed and offered Lincoln a placating smile.

'Lincoln, take some advice. I have no idea what you said to Curtis and neither will anyone else, but you've got a great reputation. Curtis ain't exactly got much of a reputation worth speaking of. People will be inclined to believe you, but only if you avoid squabbling in the road like that.'

'Point taken,' Lincoln said with a rueful

smile. 'I'll avoid Curtis from now on and just let the gossip die out.'

'That might be difficult with Karl Humboldt being so riled up. Most people might think he has a good reason to be aggrieved, and with Jack Porter still around, take some more advice, Lincoln. You need to avoid trouble, so leave town for a while.'

'You ordering me to stop investigating Ben's murder?'

'Even with a man being hanged for doing it, I don't reckon I could order you to do that, but I can ask you to take my advice. Doc Thoreau still has Lenox Devere's body and his family could do with getting it back. When you return, everything should have calmed down and you can get back to ... to tying up any loose ends.'

Lincoln searched Ellison's blank eyes, wondering if he was trying to tell him something by encouraging him to take Lenox's body to Black Point. Ellison was sure to know Lenox was in the photograph and to be aware of the possible link between his death and the recent events here.

'All right,' Lincoln said, 'I'll take the body up to Black Point and stay out of trouble for a while.'

CHAPTER 8

With the coffin containing Lenox Devere's body sitting on the back of the wagon behind him, Lincoln headed out of Independence.

At first he took the most direct route, heading around the bluff to go past Sheriff Pringle's house, then along the river where he'd fished out Lenox's body a few days ago. Before the town disappeared behind the bluff he stopped and looked back.

As he couldn't question Jack Porter or Karl Humboldt, leaving town for a while was a good idea, especially as it'd let him follow up his only remaining lead. But he couldn't shake off a nagging worry. Both Judge Murphy and Mayor Ellison, two men whom he'd trusted unthinkingly up until today, had urged, almost demanded, that he drop the investigation and both of them were in the photograph.

As he considered ulterior motives for their actions, his thoughts dwelt on the mayor's encouragement of him to leave town and deal with Lenox Devere's body. He might have been helping him move the investigation on in a secretive manner. On the other hand, Karl Humboldt had said he would exact revenge. Doing that in town where there would be plenty of witnesses would be difficult, but there would be plenty of convenient places for him to launch an ambush on the journey to Black Point.

So when Lincoln set off behind the bluff he trundled the wagon over hard ground and finally over rock, ensuring he left no tracks. Then he took an abrupt turn towards the bluff and drove the wagon into a gully. When he'd stowed the wagon out of sight from the river, he jumped down and hurried to the mouth of the gully to look out and await developments.

An hour passed without anyone passing between the bluff and the river. Although Lincoln was a patient man, he was beginning to think he might have been acting in a paranoid manner when he saw three riders heading along beside the river. They were taking the route he would have taken if he hadn't headed to the gully.

When they were closer he confirmed they were the Humboldt brothers. They passed without giving any sign that they'd worked out where he'd gone and carried on riding. They might have been looking out for him leaving town, or maybe someone had told them he'd left, or maybe even the mayor had let them know. Whatever their reason had been for following him, Lincoln still waited for another hour then took the wagon out of the gully.

When he set off he travelled downriver, at first going in the opposite direction to Black Point, before fording the river some fifteen miles lower down and doubling back.

The journey to Black Point would normally take less than a day, but with Lincoln taking a cautious and circuitous route it took him two days. That time passed without incident and without him seeing the Humboldt brothers again. The extra travelling time let him ponder. Each night he took out the faded photograph and stared at it as if it might suddenly yield up a clue as to who was behind the recent spate of killings.

The description of the picture Curtis had given him helped him to make out a blurred outline of someone at the back of the picture, which he presumed was the hanging man. Despite finding no further clues in it, he was in a hopeful frame of mind when he approached Black Point.

He came across sporadic homesteaders and asked each person he met if they knew of Lenox Devere. Everybody answered in the same way. They looked at the coffin and asked if Lenox was in it and on receiving confirmation that he was they didn't show any remorse or sadness. Several went so far as to smile and say it was about time.

One man summed up the general feeling.

'Was he murdered?' he asked.

'Yes,' Lincoln said.

'Not surprised. You here to investigate it?'

'I am.'

'Then you got yourself a tough task. I know dozens of people who could have done it without losing a minute's sleep afterwards.'

'Know of anyone who'd worry less than most?'

At this point the man saw that Lincoln was serious about conducting an inquiry and he quietened, limiting himself to giving Lincoln directions to Lenox's widow, Sarah Devere.

From the information Lincoln pieced together from each person he spoke to, Lenox had been a violent and drunken man who had been especially rough in dealing with his wife. So when Lincoln arrived at the trading post that she was now running on her own, he expected her to be a downtrodden and defeated woman. Instead, the woman who came out and hailed him did so with a cheery wave, as she probably did to all travellers. Even the years of hard-living she must have endured at Lenox's hands hadn't destroyed her beauty nor her huge and open smile. And from his high position Lincoln couldn't help but look down her low-bodice dress.

She gave him what sounded like her standard sales spiel about the wares she had available, all done in a cheerful manner, until Lincoln's sombre expression and a glance at the coffin curtailed her pleasantries.

'You taking that coffin far?' she asked, narrowing her blue eyes.

'I'm not taking it any further,' Lincoln said, then paused to let his comment register. 'I'm afraid I have some bad news for you, Sarah.'

She took a longer look at the coffin. 'That bad news had better not be that Lenox isn't in that coffin because I couldn't cope with hearing that.'

'It is him.'

She closed her eyes and placed a hand to

her chest, breathing deeply. Lincoln thought that despite her comment she might still be masking her shock but when she opened her eyes they were lively and twinkling and when she came over to the wagon she even gave a short skip.

'How did he die?'

'Found him in the river near Independence with a bullet in his chest.'

'Suppose that was a fitting end. It's been a long time coming.'

'I gather from your comments that you ain't exactly sad this happened,' Lincoln said, letting his low tone register some irritation, 'but a man has still died and–'

'A man!' she screeched, her contented mood ending in a moment. 'That sure don't describe Lenox Devere. He was an animal in a man's skin and I'll sleep easier every night knowing I don't ever have to suffer having his dirty hands all over me again.'

She leaned over the back of the wagon and spat on the coffin.

Although Lincoln was sure Lenox Devere's murder fitted into recent events in Independence, he now wondered whether Sarah's reaction suggested she could have been the one who had killed him.

'That aside, a man has still been murdered

and I need to find out everything I can about him and see if I can work out what happened.'

'I can't see why anyone would waste their time over him.' She huffed and complained some more before with a roll of her shoulders and a long sigh she got her feelings under control. She offered him her pleasant smile again. 'But I can see you're a good man. I'll tell you everything I can.'

Lincoln nodded and jumped down from the wagon.

'You can start by telling me when you last saw him.'

She bit her lip and fiddled with her sleeves while taking a more sombre look at the coffin.

'I will answer your questions but I'd prefer not to talk about him right now. I guess I am a bit shocked, after all.'

Lincoln accepted her answer with a grunt.

'And,' she continued, gesturing at the post, 'as I could do with some help in burying him, perhaps you'd like to enjoy some food and rest. If there's one thing I'm renowned for it's my hospitality.'

There was something odd in the way she said 'hospitality', and the way she smiled at him then fluffed her hair made Lincoln think that despite the closeness of her husband's body, she was flirting with him.

Three hours later, with his belly full and the third tankard of rough ale dulling his senses, he was sure.

He sat at a table in a room at the back of the trading post with her sitting opposite him and leaning forward so he had a good view of her half-exposed bosom while she continually smiled at him.

'It's time to tell me,' he said, not for the first time, as she refilled his tankard, 'what happened between you and Lenox.'

'Lenox is a long, long story,' she said, her eyes glazed, her breathing heavy, and her words slightly slurred by the liquor. 'And none of it is a nice subject for a pleasant evening like this. Talk to me about something else. I always enjoy the company of a lawman.'

Lincoln had an inkling of an idea. 'Have you ever met Sheriff Ben Pringle?'

She winced and slumped back in her chair. 'I have … met him, several times.'

Lincoln caught her hesitation. 'Did he ever come out here to see you?'

'Now you're being as inquisitive as Ben was.' She slapped his arm playfully, but then firmed her jaw and frowned. When she spoke again her tone was serious. 'But perhaps you're right. I should tell you about the man who killed Lenox.'

Lincoln noted how she had suddenly changed the subject, but if she was going to distract him from talking about Ben by revealing this piece of information, he didn't mind.

'You mean *suspect?*'

'No,' she said, 'I know who did it.'

'And his name?' He waited for her to answer, but she remained silent and guessing the reason for her sudden reticence he continued: 'Just tell me your story. It'll be hard to prove anything when all I'm likely to get is your word on what happened.'

'I will tell you about him, but not his name. I don't want you to go after him.' She snuffled. 'He doesn't deserve that.'

'I may have to find and question him, but I promise you I'll be fair.'

'I can tell you're a good man, just like ... like the man who killed Lenox.' She stared at her hands for several moments, then with a deep breath to gather her courage she continued. 'Every month Lenox used to go away. I don't know where he went but I didn't care. It let me earn a living and I sure didn't miss his drunken rages. But a woman living on her own can get awful lonely, if you know what I mean.'

'I do.'

'This man arrived and stayed with me for a while.'

Lincoln waited a respectful length of time before he ventured the obvious question.

'And was this man Ben Pringle?'

'No.' She offered a smile. 'Not this time anyhow, but this man had received a letter from Ben, and he knew the two of us were ... were friends. He was nervous about going to see him, but I told him Ben often came to see me and so he decided to wait for him here. While he waited we got real friendly and he was nice to me.'

She sighed, her eyes twinkling, perhaps as she recalled a pleasant memory.

'I reckon I know what you're trying to tell me. You and this man had a relationship, Lenox came back earlier than you expected, there was trouble.'

'That sums up what happened. The man ran away and Lenox chased after him. I expected Lenox to come back and take out his anger on me, but he never returned.'

'So you didn't see this man kill Lenox?'

'I just saw him riding off with Lenox hotfoot on his tail.' She pointed eastwards.

'They went towards the river.'

'And did this man strike you as someone who would kill?'

'When he was with me he was a gentle and kind man, but the hideous mood Lenox was in when he left meant he would either kill or be killed. I'm just glad it was be killed. I sent word down to Ben that I needed help, but he never replied.' She looked away, tears welling. 'I heard later that he didn't respond because he'd been killed.'

'And is it possible that Lenox or even this other man killed Ben?'

She raised her eyebrows, appearing shocked at the idea.

'No.'

'And did your friend return?'

'No. I assume he's still running after what he did.'

'Sarah,' he said, lowering his voice to a serious tone, 'I believe your story, but the problem is it's full of missing details and assumptions, and to bring this to an end I need some facts. I'll only get those if I find your friend. I need a name.'

She lowered her head, sighing. She didn't move again for almost a minute, but then with a shrug, as if she'd suddenly reached a decision, she looked up, and she was smiling. She leaned forward and licked her lips, her former flirtatious mood returning.

'And what would you do to get that name?'

'I would be grateful.'

'The only question on my mind is how grateful.' She raised her eyebrows and leaned forward a little more. 'It's been two long weeks since my friend left and I've been starved of affection, if you know what I mean.'

Lincoln knew exactly what she meant. He was minded to refuse her obvious offer and demand her co-operation, but the last week had been a tough one and like her, he had to admit he was feeling starved of affection.

'I believe I do,' he said. He placed a hand behind her neck and drew her closer. 'Perhaps I should show you how grateful I can be. Then we can talk about this man.'

Several hours later Lincoln lay on her bed, sprawled and sated. The shutters were open and the moon was out casting warming light over their entwined bodies.

Lincoln had avoided mentioning again the reason he had come here, waiting for her to volunteer the information. For the last half-hour she had been quiet aside from her shallow breathing, suggesting she was dozing, and so Lincoln was letting himself drift into a pleasant sleep when she spoke and gave him the name he wanted.

Her voice was low as she whispered the name and as he'd already considered the possibility of this man being involved, for a moment he wasn't sure she was answering his question.

'This is the man who stayed with you on his way to see Sheriff Pringle, then killed Lenox?' he asked, formally stating the situation to be sure he hadn't misunderstood.

'Yes,' she said. 'Sheckley Dolby killed my husband.'

'And you don't know why Ben had written to him?'

'Other than he wanted ... he wanted his help, no.'

Lincoln caught the caution in her tone, but he could accept that having given him the name she would be concerned with how Lincoln would use that information. He reached off the bed to his jacket and dragged the photograph out of his pocket.

'This is faded and it'll be hard to see in the moonlight, but...'

'Sheckley had a photograph,' she mused, peering over his shoulder. 'And from here it looks like it was the same one.'

She took it from him and peered at it, squinting in the poor light, then nodded.

'And did Sheckley say anything about it?'

'No. I only found it in his jacket after he left – he did leave in a hurry. He even left in some of Lenox's clothes.'

'And do you still have the picture?'

'I do.'

Lincoln sighed with relief. Although this picture was becoming increasingly important in working out what was happening, he had resigned himself to never actually seeing it.

'Show it to me.'

She giggled, her former good mood returning.

'I will,' she said, 'but first you'll have to show me just how grateful you can be.'

CHAPTER 9

Lincoln sat outside at a bench by the door, enjoying the warmth of the morning along with a mug of coffee.

Sarah was inside the post pottering around. He hadn't mentioned the photograph since awakening, being content to let her provide it voluntarily. Sure enough, before he'd finished his drink, she came outside with a picture clutched to her chest.

'Before I give you this,' she said, 'tell me the truth. Did you come here to find out who killed Lenox, or because of this picture?'

Sarah's perceptive question made Lincoln smile.

'I guess it was a bit of both. Several of the people in that picture have been murdered recently and I'm trying to work out why.'

'Understood.' She held out the picture for him to take then headed inside, leaving him to finally see it for himself.

He looked at the reverse side, steeling himself before he saw the actual picture.

This let him see that someone, presumably Sheckley, had written a date on the back of the picture, 8 May 1882, possibly the date of the hanging. Then he turned it over.

Before coming to Independence he had seen several photographs before, but they had always been simple posed pictures. Often they were of people sitting and looking at the camera. When he'd worked for the railroad, he'd seen ones that had depicted people working on the tracks or standing before a train. But no matter how posed those pictures had been, they were always depictions of welcome events with people facing momentous occasions in their lives and so dressed up in their finery.

That was not the case with this picture, a picture that was pretty much as Curtis had described it to him.

Seven men stood before a saloon, each man standing with a belligerent stance, some with guns drawn, others with rifles held aloft. All the men had stern glares that reached out of the picture and projected their attitude into the viewer.

Sheriff Ben Pringle stood at one end of the line of men. He had folded his arms and was the only man who was not brandishing a weapon. Despite knowing it wouldn't be the case, Lincoln had imagined seeing him as he had been on the day he had ridden off and left him sitting in his chair. But this picture had been taken ten years ago and so Ben wasn't that much older than Lincoln was now.

From most of the men Lincoln detected arrogance, perhaps even delight, but not from Ben. Lincoln understood the reason behind his stern expression because the feelings he would have been having were the same as his own would be in the same situation – disgust.

Ben would have drawn in Lincoln's gaze and kept it if it'd hadn't been for the object of his disgust. Behind them and dangling from the saloon sign was a hanging man.

Although the other men had their features clearly presented, this man's face was blurred. Perhaps it was a trick of the light that made his face appear as if it were a mask, a skull even.

Lincoln leaned forward, searching for more information in the picture. He didn't recognize the saloon and he was fairly sure it hadn't been taken in Independence. He also surmised that the men lining up before the camera had all had a part to play in bringing this man to his grisly end.

Aside from the line of men the only thing to look at was the dead man. He peered more closely at him but he couldn't decide whether the man was wearing a mask or not. He hoped he had been because then that would provide a possible clue as to what was happening. Maybe a friend or relative of the dead man had obtained the mask and was wearing it while getting his revenge on the men in the picture.

'Did it help?' Sarah asked from the doorway, breaking him out of his reverie.

'Some.'

'Was that working out why people are dying in Independence, or how you might find Sheckley Dolby?'

'The first.' Lincoln watched her sigh with relief. Despite the intimacy they'd shared last night and her feelings for Ben, he gathered she still cared for Sheckley. 'I've promised you I'll be fair when I question him about why he had to kill Lenox, but I now reckon he's also in danger. If you can tell me anything about him and where he went, now would be the time to do it.'

'I'm sorry,' she said, shaking her head.

Lincoln believed her, but he also couldn't dismiss the thought that Sheckley might help him find the masked man because

Sheckley could be that man. To work out whether that was the case he needed to know why all the people in this picture were in it. The judge, the mayor, and the lawman, he could understand, but not the others.

'Do you know anyone who might know anything about this photograph?'

She smiled. 'In fact, I do.'

Lincoln returned the smile, but then shook his head and raised a hand.

'I can't make you talk like I did last night. I have to act quickly.'

'A pity,' she said, then told him a name.

Five minutes later Lincoln was riding away from the trading post and heading for Black Point, after having promised to return later and help her bury Lenox.

When he arrived in town he found that it was a bustling settlement, about half the size of Independence. Lincoln soon located the mercantile Sarah had directed him to and dismounted outside, then stopped with a hand still holding on to his horse's reins.

Down the road was a saloon and outside were three horses he recognized – the Humboldt brothers were in town.

Lincoln had stopped worrying about them. They knew of his destination but he'd expected them to have become bored with looking for him and so to have returned to Independence by now. But he had a mission to complete and so he headed into the mercantile.

The place had a wide range of merchandise along with a prominent advertisement for a service that nobody in Independence provided: RUFUS WAINWRIGHT'S PHOTOGRAPHIC EMPORIUM.

'Come in, come in,' Rufus, a man with a bristling moustache and a cheery demeanour, said. 'I have no doubt such a fine upstanding man as yourself will make a fine subject.'

'Obliged,' Lincoln said, then introduced himself.

Rufus rocked back on his heels to appraise Lincoln.

'I've always thought the lawmen I've captured have looked so dignified, but it's been a great sorrow for me that until now a subject as noble as yourself hasn't come into my little emporium.'

Lincoln gritted his teeth in irritation.

'Quit the flattery.'

'I like a man who doesn't waste time.' Rufus raised a finger and winked. 'And you'll like my competitive rates and are sure to enjoy a memento you'll want to treasure for ever. Now, what pose would–?'

'Don't get too hopeful. I'm not interested in having my picture taken. I'm more interested in a photograph you took some time ago.'

Rufus tucked a thumb into his waistcoat pocket and held out his other hand.

'Show it to me and perhaps I might still be able to interest you in one just like it.'

'I hope not. I don't ever want to see another picture like this one.'

Lincoln withdrew the picture and held it out to Rufus, who took it, his face wreathed in a smile that died as soon as his eyes had focused on the picture. Rufus sighed then walked over to the window to consider the picture in full light.

'Ah,' he said, 'that photograph. What do you want to know about it?'

'Seven men are in that picture. One is the mayor of Independence, one is the judge, one just lost his business, one might be wanted for murder, the other three are dead.'

'Three? I'd heard about Wesley Jameson and Sheriff Pringle.'

'Lenox Devere died last week. For some reason a picture taken ten years ago is now leading to a spate of murders and I want to know why. So we'll start with the simplest question – who is the dead man?'

'The person hanging from the saloon sign was Quincy Allen.'

Lincoln shook his head. 'Never heard of him. What did he do, and where did he do it?'

Rufus didn't reply as he looked through the window, only a sigh and his hunched shoulders betraying his feelings. Then he turned to Lincoln, handed the picture back to him, and went to the door.

'Perhaps it'd be more useful to you if I just showed you,' he said.

Lincoln followed him outside. He glanced down the road to confirm that the Humboldt brothers were still in the saloon. Then they headed out of town, going south broadly towards Independence.

Two hours later they stood amidst the remnants of a town that, according to the mouldering sign which dangled from a rusty nail on a leaning post, had once been called Destitution. According to Rufus, when the original homesteaders had settled the area they'd set up here. But the town had soon outgrown the limited resources. So they'd either headed north to the fertile land around Black Point, or south towards the railroad and Independence, leaving Destitution to become another soon-to-be-forgotten collection of rotting shacks that could have become a town if it'd had better luck.

Only five identifiable buildings remained and one of those was the original trading post. Its frame stood at an angle, only the saloon beside it stopping it from falling over as it awaited a kindly wind to come along and flatten it.

From down the road, the low sun cast long shadows behind the skeletal remains of the other buildings, decay ensuring Lincoln couldn't work out what purpose they had once served.

If the saloon had had a sign, Lincoln couldn't see it, but despite the rotted timber, this was clearly the place in the photograph.

'What happened here?' Lincoln asked.

'Quincy Allen happened,' Rufus said, then led him from the saloon. He counted his paces until he came to a scrappy patch of grass and within that patch there were three overgrown mounds.

'Graves?' Lincoln watched Rufus nod, then knelt to look for any sign of who these people had been, but time had eroded away any inscribed names. But he could just make out a date on one of the markers of 14 June 1882. 'This is when they died?'

Rufus furrowed his brow as he pondered, then shrugged.

'I guess it must have been.'

Lincoln didn't comment on the fact that this date was a month after the date on the back of the photograph.

'Which one is Quincy Allen's grave?'

'He ain't buried here – not after what he did.'

'And what did he do?'

'Killed these men. Stanley, James and Luke Allen died in that very saloon. They were playing poker when the saloon owner left them, but then–'

'Wesley Jameson by any chance?'

'Sure. They were enjoying themselves until Quincy joined them. Quincy reckoned himself to be a fine poker player, but he always cheated, even when playing with his own brothers. When Wesley returned later, the three men lay around a half-dealt hand and Quincy had hightailed it out of there.'

'But he didn't get away with it for long?'

'Nope. It took some effort though. Sheriff Ben Pringle couldn't find him, but Paul Ellison had just become mayor in Independence and he promised he wouldn't rest until he brought Quincy Allen to justice. The men in the picture all had a hand in catching him. And everybody rejoiced when he was swinging from the saloon sign.'

'Why take a picture of it?'

'It was Ellison's first victory of his administration and he put the picture up everywhere as a deterrent to show what would happen to anyone who broke the law. You can agree or disagree with what he did, but everyone got the message and the place was law-abiding afterwards.'

'What did each of the men do?'

'The mayor organized the hunt. The judge found Quincy guilty. The sheriff ran the case. Billy Stone bankrolled the reward money. Wesley was the nearest they had to a witness.'

'And the other two, Sheckley and Lenox?'

'Sheckley was the bounty hunter who brought Quincy in.' Rufus sighed. 'Lenox was the only one who enjoyed his task. He was the executioner.'

'And now the men in that picture are dying. Any idea who could be killing them?'

'I find it hard to believe someone could have a grudge against them. Quincy didn't exactly make any friends with what he did here.'

Lincoln thanked him, but before mounting up to ride back to Independence, he withdrew the picture from his jacket and looked at it again. Then he paced to the spot where the people in the picture would have stood. He judged that they had been twenty or so yards from the saloon. Then he looked towards the graves.

'I ain't got much experience with taking photographs,' he said. 'But I judge you'd have had to have stood right in the middle of those graves to take this picture.'

Rufus shrugged. 'I can't remember exactly, but perhaps they hadn't been buried yet.'

'And did Quincy wear a mask?'

Rufus smiled. 'I can see you're intrigued by the new science of photography. The subject has to stand still when I capture his image or the representation gets distorted, but Quincy wasn't exactly brave at the end. No matter what anyone says about him, that's the truth of his death.'

Lincoln nodded then turned away from facing the graves to take in the scene for one last time before he returned to the trading post.

A gunshot rang out. Lincoln heard the slug clatter into the saloon behind him. He was several yards from his horse and had to make a split-second decision of whether to hightail it out of town or head for cover and fight it out. He saw movement ahead in the bushes beyond the graves and heard the rustling of several people advancing on him. He decided that if he tried to leave he would be too obvious a target. So he batted Rufus's arm to get his attention then pointed to the saloon.

They set off, but the assailants had got themselves organized and a volley of bullets whined all around them and encouraged them to run as fast as they could before they dived through the open doorway. Lincoln rolled to the side and crouched then looked around, gauging his chances of making a stand. The saloon was derelict but the rotting wood did provide some cover.

'Keep your head down,' Lincoln ordered before he ventured a glance through the window himself. He again saw movement, this time seeing three people moving to positions closer to the saloon.

He appraised the opposition he faced until gunshots scythed through the window and forced him to duck. From the variety of angles at which the slugs cannoned through the window and crashed into the walls, Lincoln judged that his assailants had spread out.

'Who are they?' Rufus asked.

'The Humboldt brothers from Independence,' Lincoln said, 'but don't worry, you'll be safe with me.'

'I don't doubt it.' Rufus frowned. 'What a pity I left my camera back in Black Point. This situation would make a fine picture.'

Lincoln acknowledged Rufus's humorous comment with a grunt, then edged along below the window. He stood at the side. He ventured out and fired twice, then darted back when the expected gunfire blasted into the wall around the window. Again he'd seen the brothers and again they were closer to the saloon, now aiming to come at him from several directions.

'So you finally got the courage to take me on,' Lincoln shouted, more to hear their responses and judge their positions than to taunt them.

'Yeah,' Karl Humboldt shouted, from around twenty yards away and to the left of the window, perhaps as he sought to come around the side of the saloon. 'You'll pay for what you did to our brother.'

With the front wall of the saloon being the only available cover, Lincoln decided to seek a better position.

He gestured for Rufus to join him. Then they crawled away from the front wall and beyond the extent of the rotting saloon floor to the scrubby ground beyond. Lincoln saw little in the way of cover but he gestured for Rufus to lie on his belly and make himself as small a target as possible then joined him, lying a few yards to his side.

The brothers would risk either coming through the saloon door or around the sides, but from whichever angle they came Lincoln would now be able to see them first. He roved his gun back and forth, biding his time.

A minute passed during which time he heard the brothers shouting instructions to each other. He couldn't hear all those instructions, but he gathered they'd secured his and Rufus's horses and so had ensured they wouldn't be going anywhere. He also detected confidence in their exchanged comments. Lincoln vowed to ensure that that confidence would be misplaced.

A volley of gunshots rang out, all coming from the left of the saloon. Then a single shot came from the right. Lincoln presumed they were trying to confuse him as to the direction from which they'd make their move. He instructed Rufus to keep down, then awaited developments. Another volley of shots rang out, followed by an agonized cry, then a thud.

'Show yourself!' Karl shouted from the other side of the saloon wall, the angry demand making Lincoln glance at Rufus to see he'd raised his head.

'Help's arrived?' Rufus asked.

'It certainly sounds like it.' Lincoln shrugged. 'But then again maybe that's what it was supposed to sound like.'

Lincoln heard another shout followed by a burst of gunfire then shuffling and movement, which sounded to Lincoln like the brothers mounting their horses. Then those horses thundered out of town. Through the skeletal remains of the standing buildings Lincoln caught fleeting glimpses of the horses hurrying away and the trail dust billowed up.

'Now,' Rufus said, 'if they're trying to distract us by making it sound like they're fleeing, they're sure doing it well.'

Lincoln acknowledged Rufus's comment with a smile, then jumped to his feet. He told Rufus to stay down and made his cautious way to the front of the saloon. He still wasn't convinced that what he thought had happened had in fact happened. Nobody who might be inclined to help him should have been aware of where he was, and it was just as likely that two of the brothers had left town noisily, leaving one behind to ambush him.

Accordingly, he glanced out the door at the fleeing riders. They were too far away for Lincoln to see anything other than a cloud of dust.

Lincoln waited until the town descended into quiet, then waited another five minutes. Still he heard nothing, so he accepted that if this were a trap he would have to make a move to spring it or he'd never get to leave town. He moved into the saloon doorway, slipped outside and pressed his back to the wall. The road was deserted.

He paced out into the road, keeping the plains where the brothers had hidden themselves earlier ahead, the scrubby bushes with the graves to his left and the buildings to his right. Then he steadily paced down the road. He had passed the saloon when a slight sound gave him the first inkling that his cautious approach was the right thing to do. A faint sound came from the trading post beside the saloon.

It was just a rustling and Lincoln avoided reacting to it, watching the post from the corner of his eye while walking onwards.

Then he saw the splatter of blood on the ground outside the post and the blood smeared down the doorframe and he stopped believing this was a trap.

He hurried across the road, pressed himself to the wall beside the door, then darted inside, his gun thrust out. He homed in on the huddled form lying beside the door. Lincoln went over and rolled the person on to his back with the toe of his boot to see that it was Wilhelm Humboldt, the youngest brother after Alex's demise. A reddened hole in his chest confirmed that Heinrich Humboldt would soon be the youngest surviving brother.

'Who?' Lincoln asked.

Wilhelm moved for his gun, his action slow, letting Lincoln kick his hand away long before it reached the gun. Then Wilhelm sneered up at him, a bubble of blood on his lips.

'I ain't talking, Lincoln.'

'I'm the only one who can hear your last words. Your brothers didn't stay around for you.'

Wilhelm twitched, his action perhaps being an attempt at a shrug.

'Don't know no name.' A spasm contorted Wilhelm's face and his body racked backwards. When he spoke again his voice was barely audible. 'He was just death.'

Then his head lolled to the side.

Lincoln climbed out of the shallow grave and stretched his back. The ground was so hard it'd taken him three hours to scrape out a few feet of earth for Lenox Devere's grave. Sarah had piled rocks beside the hole, then she stood back with an odd expression on her face that Lincoln thought might be sadness, or perhaps guilt because she didn't feel sad.

'Do you want me to leave you alone for a while?' he asked.

'No,' she said. 'I've said all the curses I want to say. Let's just get him in the hole and get this over with.'

'If that's what you want.'

Lincoln slipped his hands under the coffin preparing to drag it to the hole. It wasn't heavy but it was unwieldy and to retain some dignity for the deceased man he hoped she'd help him. Instead, she just stared at the coffin. So Lincoln shifted his weight and prepared to move it on his own, but she slowly raised a hand.

'Wait,' she said. 'Open the coffin first.'

Lincoln lowered the coffin then stood back and shook his head.

'I wouldn't advise that. He'd been in the water for a week.'

'I know that, but I have to see.'

Lincoln understood the need some people have to see that a person is dead before they're prepared to accept it, so he asked her to stand further back, then slipped the spade beneath the lid and prised it open. Only two nails were holding the lid down and when he'd dragged them away he flipped the lid to the ground.

He noted that the undertaker had wrapped the shrunken body in cloth before he looked at her with his eyebrows raised.

'Is that enough?'

'No. I need to see him.' She produced a knife then wrapped her shawl over her nose and mouth before she went to her knees beside the coffin.

Lincoln expected her to slit open the cloth around the face so that she could see what was left of Lenox's features but instead she felt along the side of the body to locate the arm. Then she traced along to the right hand, which the undertaker had placed on the body's chest. She cut through the cloth, then peeled it away to reveal a blackened and bloated hand, predators having eaten away stretches of skin to leave protruding bones.

A sob escaped her lips and she jumped to her feet, tearing the shawl away. She swirled round looking away from the body with her knuckles pressed to her lips. Lincoln assumed she had now seen what she'd wanted to see, so he placed the lid back on the coffin, then joined her.

He wrapped an arm around her shoulders and tried to hug her but she pushed herself away from him.

'Why did you look at his hand?' he asked.

She didn't reply immediately and when she did speak there was sorrow and perhaps even fear in her voice.

'Five years ago Lenox got into a fight with a man from Black Point, Brian Wheeler. Lenox tried to stab him but Brian turned the knife back on him and cut off the top of the smallest finger of his right hand.'

Lincoln understood what she was suggesting. He refused to let that thought worry him and asked the obvious question.

'Does that corpse have part of a finger missing?'

'No. All its fingers are whole.' She turned to him with her watering eyes opened wide. 'It must be Sheckley Dolby's body.'

Lincoln nodded. 'And that means Lenox Devere is still out there, somewhere.'

CENTRAL WEST LIBRARIES

CHAPTER 10

During his time as a lawman Lincoln had been on numerous manhunts and had sometimes covered vast distances, but he'd found that not all hunts required the hunter to travel. Sometimes it was just a matter of staying where he was and waiting for the hunted to find him.

This was just such an occasion.

Lenox's habits were mysterious but predictable. He went away each month, presumably visiting nearby towns on a drunken meander. When he returned he would take out his anger on Sarah but would then settle down, even helping her with the chores in running the trading post.

For a while their life together would be quiet but then he would become impatient again until eventually the wanderlust would overcome him and he'd leave, returning again after a few weeks.

Last time he'd returned to find Sheckley in the trading post with Sarah and he'd left to pursue him. That'd been several weeks ago, so Sarah reckoned it was just a matter of time before he returned.

So Lincoln waited. He had to admit his motivations in taking this course of action were mixed. Although Sarah was pleasant company, even with the threat of the returning Lenox overhanging them, Lincoln also reckoned Lenox had probably killed Ben Pringle. He had gathered that Sarah was free with her favours and that Lenox didn't take kindly to this. Ben's monthly visits to Black Point were to see Sarah while Lenox was away, so he surmised that Lenox had decided to take revenge on him, as he had done to Sheckley.

The questions as to whether the letter Ben had written to Sheckley was to warn him about the masked man, whether Lenox was that masked man, and how the situation fitted into Quincy Allen's fate, Lincoln couldn't answer. But he resolved to solve one problem at a time.

Four days passed without incident until on the fifth night after discovering that Lenox was still alive Lincoln heard a noise outside. Sarah was lying in bed and Lincoln was sitting up in a chair as he had done since burying Sheckley. A solitary lamp turned down low provided more shadow than light.

A traveller looking to use the trading post could have made the noise, but it was long past midnight and this possibility was less likely than the more worrying one.

Lincoln told Sarah to stay in bed, then went to the window and listened. He heard the horses in the corral shifting around, something clearly having spooked them, so he gestured to Sarah to extinguish the light, offered her a comforting word, then quietly opened the shutters and climbed out of the window.

The low half-moon provided enough light for Lincoln to see the corral. He confirmed that the horses were restless, so he took the long route around the post to the front, venturing a glance around every corner before moving on. He had traversed three sides of the building and was preparing to look around the last corner when he heard a noise.

It was just a pebble skittering across the ground ahead, but it was rare for anything to make that sound naturally. In Lincoln's experience that sort of noise only came when someone threw a stone to attract another's attention. And usually the person who had thrown the stone was nowhere near the actual sound.

Lincoln doubled back, keeping his back to the wall and walking sideways. He glanced around the corner of the building, saw nothing ahead, then slipped around and hurried on to the next corner. A thud sounded beyond the corner, but despite this noise possibly being another distraction, Lincoln looked round the corner to see a sack of corn lying on the ground, dust rising around it.

Lincoln looked up, expecting to see the person who had pushed the sack off the roof, and found himself looking straight up into a man's face. Darkness shrouded his features and before Lincoln could turn his gun on him, the man jumped down and dropped on him, flattening him to the ground.

Lincoln squirmed, aiming to throw the man away, but solid metal thudded into the side of his head with a sickening jar. Lincoln tried to struggle but found that his limbs had no strength and they wouldn't obey him. Then the night sky appeared to swim around him before unconsciousness overcame him.

A timeless period passed in which uneasy dreams flitted across Lincoln's mind until with a start he awoke from his unconscious slumber.

It was light. He was lying on his side. He groggily orientated himself while slowly recalling what had happened to him. A man, possibly Lenox, had knocked him out, then kidnapped him and taken him away from the post. Now he was lying on the ground. He was in a rocky hollow and perhaps some distance from the trading post.

Without moving, to avoid alerting Lenox if he was looking at him, he looked around, but he failed to see anyone in his limited field of vision. He thought it was unlikely that he had been left alone, but in case that was what had happened he tried to sit and discovered that his hands were tied together. When he tugged his hands didn't move. A glance over his shoulder confirmed what had been done to him.

Behind him and hammered deep into the ground was a thick stake. His hands were bound and a rope secured him to the stake. Lincoln stood and shook the rope, discovering it was about twenty feet long, but he also discovered something more worrying – his captor was still here. The man was sitting on the side of the hollow watching him, twenty yards away. In the shadow beneath the man's hat Lincoln saw some of the man's face, and it was a cold and white visage that resembled a skull – surely a mask.

'Why have you brought me here?' Lincoln said, holding his hands as wide as his tight bonds would let him.

Lincoln waited but he didn't get an answer from the silent and enigmatic figure.

'Are you Lenox Devere?'

No answer.

'Then who are you?' Lincoln persisted.

No answer.

'What are you planning to do?'

Lincoln took a deep breath after a few seconds of silence.

'What did you do to Sarah?'

He still didn't get an answer and accepting he was unlikely to get a response no matter what he asked, he asked one final question, the one that bemused him the most.

'I reckon it could only have been you who saved me from the Humboldt brothers back in Destitution. So why have you captured me now?'

The masked man didn't answer this either, but he did get to his feet. He faced Lincoln with the blank mask of his face staring down at him, then turned and slowly paced up the side of the hollow. Lincoln shouted taunts and threats at his receding back, but the man didn't react and slowly he disappeared from view over the rim, leaving Lincoln alone in the hollow.

Lincoln then wasted no time in turning his thoughts to how he could escape before the masked man returned. Both the stake and the rope were thick and when Lincoln headed over to the stake and experimentally kicked it, the wood returned a solid sound.

Lincoln played the rope out to its utmost then walked in a circle around the stake but from all angles he couldn't see beyond the hollow and so couldn't tell where he was. It was possible that the masked man had secured him here then left him to meet a lingering end. Despite this possibility, Lincoln decided to keep his strength by not shouting out to attract the attention of anyone who happened to be nearby, especially as he viewed that possibility as being remote.

So he lay on the ground before the stake and alternated between using the only two possible ways he had to free himself. He braced himself then kicked the stake with both heels. When his legs began to ache, he rolled on his side and scraped the rope around his wrists across the stony ground.

For the first hour neither act had any noticeable effect, but after the second hour the constant wearing on the rope started to fray the twine. The stake was as resolutely solid as ever, but if he had in fact been abandoned here, then he felt that he would be able to wear through the rope before his hunger and thirst killed him.

The sun reached its highest point then headed for Lincoln's limited horizon. All the time Lincoln measured his success in working through the rope in hair's breadths.

Long shadows were creeping across the hollow when he stopped trying to dislodge the stake and put all his efforts into wearing through the rope. He even found a stone with a sharp edge, which accelerated the fraying.

But then from the corner of his eye he noticed a shadow moving beyond the stake. He avoided reacting to it and kept himself hunched over to hide his sharp stone. He saw the shadow resolve into the forms of two men leading their horses. They were behind him and walking along the edge of the hollow while looking down at him.

They wouldn't be able to see what he was doing, but a consideration of his progress through the rope convinced him that he couldn't break through before they came down to him. So he sought to pretend that he hadn't been trying to escape and turned his head to the shadows, flinched as if he'd seen them for the first time, then turned to the people.

He had to narrow his eyes against the lowering sun but could still only make out their outlines. He shuffled backwards to place his back to the stake and watched them make their way down the side of the hollow. The first man was the masked man and he stopped half-way down and held on to both horses. The second man was taller and brawnier and he continued walking until he reached the bottom of the hollow where he stomped to a halt and glared at Lincoln. Although Lincoln had never met him before, he resembled a man he'd seen in a photograph.

It was Lenox Devere. This also meant he couldn't be the masked man, but that thought wasn't uppermost in Lincoln's mind as Lenox stared down at him with wild eyes.

'You ready to die, Lincoln?' he grunted.

Lincoln didn't think that replying would help him and he contented himself with returning Lenox's glare until Lenox snorted with derision, then advanced on him. With his arms held wide to grab his bound target, Lenox took steady paces towards him.

Lincoln backed away but then quickly had to circle round the stake when the rope tugged him to the side. Lenox grinned when he saw how Lincoln's predicament was hampering him.

As they continued to circle, Lincoln accepted that his current circling motion would only bind him to the stake, eventually. He stopped and doubled back and moved between Lenox and the stake.

But Lenox had been looking into his eyes and had anticipated his action. He darted to the left, then with a large fist delivered a stinging blow to Lincoln's cheek that sent him reeling. Lincoln rolled once then came to his feet facing Lenox. He continued to back away while flexing his jaw.

Lenox followed him, but that gave Lincoln an idea. The rope was playing out on the ground as he walked backwards and Lenox's feet were traipsing along beside the rope. So Lincoln took a significant glance at the watching masked man. This glance drew Lenox's attention away from him for a moment and let Lincoln swirl his arms to make the rope lie in a large circle on the ground.

Then he slowed the speed of his pacing, letting Lenox close on him. He reached the maximum extent of his range from the stake that he could achieve while still leaving the loop on the ground, then stopped.

Lenox continued to advance until he obligingly stepped into the loop.

Lincoln yanked back on the rope tightening it around Lenox's ankle, then tugged with all his might tumbling Lenox over. Before Lenox could right himself Lincoln was on him. He swirled the rope again and succeeded in looping a coil of rope around Lenox's neck. Then he pulled back as he dropped to his knees behind him.

He grasped a length of rope in both hands and strained, aiming to throttle Lenox. For several moments the rope bit into Lenox's neck, making him gag and squirm, but then Lenox grabbed the rope and he also began to strain. Inch by inch Lenox dragged the rope away from his neck. Lincoln's bound hands were unable to resist Lenox's superior strength and slowly Lenox opened up a loop, then shook it away from his head.

When the rope was clear of his head Lenox bent at the waist, reached back to grab Lincoln's arms and hurled him over his shoulders. Lincoln somersaulted and landed flat on his back on the hard ground, the force blasting the air from his lungs.

Lenox stood, still clutching the rope, then repaid Lincoln for his good idea by swirling the rope around Lincoln's ankle. He pulled it tight and dragged Lincoln across the ground towards the stake.

Lincoln was still groggy but he fought to right himself and just managed to force himself into a sitting position when he reached the stake. But he instantly regretted the move when Lenox turned on his heel and delivered a swinging kick to his chin that slammed Lincoln on his back.

Lincoln floundered, disorientated and groggy. He waved his arms as he ineffectually tried to ward Lenox off, but Lenox avoided his flailing arms and darted in to grab Lincoln from behind. Then he dragged Lincoln to the stake, placed his back to it, and swirled the rope over the top until he'd secured him to it.

While Lenox stood back to admire his handiwork, Lincoln shook his head, clearing his thoughts. His blurred and swimming vision gradually sharpened so that he could see the grim-faced Lenox standing over him. Lincoln tugged on his bonds, but Lenox had secured him well. He reckoned with enough time he could loosen the rope, but Lenox's blazing eyes and suffused face suggested he wasn't going to give him that time.

'Time to die, Lincoln,' he muttered, then turned on his heel, went purposefully back to his horse, and returned with his gun. He raised and straightened his arm, then aimed at Lincoln, who glared back up at him.

'Killing a lawman is a big mistake,' Lincoln said. 'First Sheckley Dolby, then me. When will this stop?'

'I'll stop when varmints like you stop abusing my wife,' Lenox roared.

'Abusing?' Lincoln snorted. 'That wasn't the way it was.'

'Quit whining. Sheckley begged for his life but it did him no good.'

'From what I've heard of Sheckley, he wouldn't beg. He really cared for Sarah.'

Lenox sneered. 'He didn't care for her or he wouldn't have done what he did.'

Lincoln considered the gun, noting that Lenox still hadn't cocked it, presumably as he waited for Lincoln either to confess to his imagined crimes or plead for his life. Lincoln would never do either.

'Done what?' he asked.

'You know what he did,' Lenox roared, his

face darkening by the moment. 'You're all the same.'

'But we weren't,' Lincoln said, his voice becoming calmer as Lenox's became more desperate. 'We were just two men who happened to stop by at the trading post while you away, and found a woman starved of affection.'

Lenox narrowed his eyes. 'What you trying to say?'

'I'm saying Sarah has needs, and just because you can't satisfy–'

'Enough!'

Lincoln reckoned that annoying Lenox by baiting him would get him killed either quickly or painfully, but at the moment he didn't have much in the way of a choice. He also started to see that in an odd way Lenox did care for Sarah and that he didn't know the reason for her activities while he was away, or wouldn't admit it to himself.

'How many more men must you kill because of her? How many have you killed?'

'Just Sheckley, and now you.' Lenox raised the gun and sighted Lincoln's chest.

'What about Sheriff Ben Pringle? Did you kill him?'

'Sheriff...' Lenox flinched back, his mouth opening wide in shock. 'What about him?'

Lincoln reckoned he'd touched a raw nerve in mentioning Ben, but he judged that he'd never be able to reason with Lenox and so he continued baiting him.

'Ben was like Sheckley. He was another man who cared for your wife. He'd been coming up to Black Point once a month for the last ten years.' Lincoln raised his eyebrows. 'You used to leave town every month, didn't you?'

Lenox roared with frustration. He thrust his arms up high, imploring the heavens to strike Lincoln down, then darted his gun hand down, but instead of firing he hurled the gun at Lincoln. The weapon flew past his cheek before skittering across the ground. Then Lenox fell to his knees and placed his forehead to the ground, bleating with what sounded like animal noises.

The truth appeared to have broken Lenox and Lincoln reckoned when he'd stopped berating himself he would either leave as a defeated man or beat him to death with his bare hands. So Lincoln tugged on his bonds, trying to free himself so he could make a run for the gun. With his hands tied around the stake he had to squirm but slowly he managed to kneel then stand as he pushed the rope up the stake behind his back. Then he levered it over the top, but before the rope could coil down to the ground Lenox looked up, and his eyes were glazed.

'Is this true?' he asked, his voice low and pained. He didn't look at the rope that was still settling on the ground. 'Did others ... others like Ben love her?'

'They did, and she them,' Lincoln said. He moved to the side so that he could see the discarded gun, judging that he could reach it before Lenox did as long as he went for it first and moved quickly.

'What can I do?' Lenox implored, again looking skyward and giving Lincoln the chance to take another pace towards the gun. 'What can I do? What can I–?'

A gunshot tore out and Lenox went spinning away to land on his side, a neat red hole marring the centre of his forehead.

Lincoln looked to the side to see that the masked man had stood up and was pacing down to them, his gun drawn and smoking. Lincoln flinched, aiming to try the long and possibly hopeless run for the discarded gun, but the man darted his gun to the side to aim it at him, giving him no choice but to give up on the attempt. Instead, Lincoln stood tall and watched him approach. Every step closer helped to confirm to Lincoln that his adversary was wearing a mask.

'What do you want?' Lincoln asked.

The masked man stopped walking. Lincoln waited for an answer but only silence greeted him.

'Why are you doing this?' Lincoln continued.

The man behind the mask continued to look down at him, the gun barrel not wavering from its steady aim at Lincoln's forehead.

'Then if you're not going to answer my questions you'll just have to shoot me.' Lincoln jutted his chin proudly, determined to die with dignity.

A flash of teeth appeared in the mask's mouth gap, suggesting that the man had smiled. Then he drew the gun back into his hand and with a twirl of the wrist dropped it back into his holster. He took steady paces backwards.

'Who are you?' Lincoln shouted after him, and this time the man stopped.

'Have you heard of the man they couldn't hang?' he said with laughter in his tone. Then he paced away, his form gradually melting into the gathering gloom.

CHAPTER 11

It took Lincoln an hour to scrape through his bonds and free himself by which time night had fallen and the masked man had long gone. It took him another hour to orient himself to the stars and find the nearest trail, and another three hours after that before he made it back to the trading post.

To his relief, Sarah was uninjured and she threw herself into his arms and sobbed. With her voice muffled as she buried her head against his shoulder she reported that she hadn't even known what had happened to him and had guessed that maybe he had gone off in pursuit of Lenox.

He told her the bad news of Lenox's eventual demise, to which she responded with the relief he'd expected.

Later, Lincoln gathered a few hours of restful sleep and in the morning they headed out to collect Lenox's body. This time they completed his burial.

After that, Lincoln had no reason to stay at the trading post. He departed for Independence, although the obliging and now relaxed Sarah promised him a warm bed and a full belly if he should ever pass this way again.

Lincoln resolved to do just that, then took his leave of her.

Late in the day he rode back into Independence. On the way, he'd pondered on what he'd learnt while he'd been in Black Point. He had resolved to talk to the surviving people in the photograph first. He asked around and found out that Billy Stone was out of town today. Nobody had seen Mayor Ellison recently. But Judge Murphy's whereabouts were familiar to everyone.

So Lincoln headed into the Rising Sun saloon. The customers quietened then glared at him; clearly Alex Humboldt's unfortunate demise was still a sore point around town. Lincoln noted that one person wasn't looking his way, and in fact the customers were giving this person a wide berth – Judge Murphy was drinking himself into a stupor at a corner table.

With the eyes of everyone in the saloon on him, Lincoln headed over to his table.

'Have you seen Mayor Ellison?' he asked, sitting opposite him.

Murphy looked up at him with bleary and red-rimmed eyes, taking an inordinate amount of time to focus on him until he eventually grunted with recognition.

'Ain't seen him much. He spends all his time in his office. Not that I can blame him. We're all hated these days after what happened to Alex Humboldt.' Murphy sniffed, then rubbed his watering eyes. 'I sentenced the wrong man to hang.'

Lincoln sat opposite him. 'What made you realize?'

'I got to thinking. Everybody blamed you, but I know the way it was.'

'Why did you do it?'

'You know why. You've been to Black Point.'

'You admitting you knew the events of ten years ago were resurfacing?'

'The truth always comes out. I should have known that.'

'And what is the truth?' Lincoln waited while Murphy downed his glass of whiskey and poured himself another, but the judge still didn't provide an answer and instead slumped down with his head lowered. 'Then tell me about the man they couldn't hang.'

'Leave me,' Murphy murmured.

'Was he Quincy Allen? Is he really dead? What actually happened ten years ago? What–?'

'Leave me!' Murphy roared, pointing with a shaking hand in the general direction of the door. When Lincoln didn't move, he grabbed the nearly empty whiskey bottle and hurled it at him. Even from so close his aim was poor and the bottle skidded across the table before smashing to the floor.

Murphy looked at the broken glass with tears brimming over, almost as if he was sad to see good whiskey go to waste. Then with as much dignity as he could muster he lurched to his feet, pushed his way past Lincoln, and weaved a path to the door.

'Who is the man they couldn't hang?' Lincoln said to Murphy's back.

Murphy stopped, confirming he'd heard the question, then continued on his way to the door. Lincoln was about to follow him, irritated now and determined to obtain an answer, but found that a man had left the bar and was considering him with interest. This in itself was unusual as everyone else was now ignoring him with studied disdain.

'You want to know about the man they couldn't hang, do you?' he said, offering a gap-toothed smile.

Lincoln nodded cautiously, then recognized the man as being a harmless old-timer, Charlie Thompson, possibly the oldest person in town, and a man who'd sell his soul to the devil if the payment came in whiskey. Lincoln nodded and followed him to the bar where he bought him a whiskey, then wasted no time in questioning him.

'Tell me about him,' he said.

'You bought me one drink and one drink only,' Charlie said, then licked his lips with a greedy glare lighting his eyes, 'and that don't mean I have to talk to the likes of you.'

'No matter what people say about me, I'm the only man who'd buy the likes of you anything. Talk or that's the only drink you'll get off me.'

'You speak plenty of sense,' Charlie said, chuckling, then downed his drink and smiled hopefully. When Lincoln had refilled the glass he continued. 'People are still calling Jack Porter that.'

'So he's still around?'

'I guess. I ain't seen him much these last few days.'

'But either way I don't mean him. I mean the previous man they couldn't hang.' Lincoln waited, then prompted: 'Quincy Allen perhaps?'

'It was him, but he got hung some ten years back so that boast didn't count for nothing.'

'Then why the boast?'

'Before they got him he thought he was above the law. Every crime that happened around these parts he was behind it. Except nobody could prove nothing. He was just too damn careful.' Charlie winked. 'Any witnesses knew what'd happen to them if they talked.'

'I understand, but eventually somebody did talk.'

'Yeah, Wesley Jameson spoke up against him, and it sure was good for everyone that he did after Quincy shot up all four of his own brothers.'

'I heard there were only three.'

Charlie considered then shrugged. 'Perhaps I remembered it wrong. It was a long time ago.'

Lincoln poured Charlie another drink, but then noticed the shadows of several people were spreading across the bar and his neck burned with the distinct impression that these people were looking at him. He turned to find that several men were standing around him. At the front was the surly form of Independence's former deputy sheriff Alan Curtis.

'You're asking an awful lot of questions,' Curtis said.

'That's what lawmen do, so you wouldn't

know that.'

'Curtis sneered, then cocked his thumb to the side, ordering Charlie to move away. Charlie didn't waste a moment in grabbing his glass and scooting down the bar.

'I know what this lawman is about to do,' Curtis said.

Lincoln noted that the men around Curtis all had the arrogant look of hired guns and that they were bunching their fists. Lincoln stood tall.

'Curtis,' he said, 'you ain't a deputy sheriff no longer and I'm minded to arrest you for getting in a real lawman's way. Now, move!'

'You can't order me do that, now that I'm not a deputy sheriff no more.' Curtis gave a huge grin. 'But that's only because I'm now a sheriff.'

Lincoln snorted. 'Who pinned a badge on you?'

'Mayor Ellison,' Curtis said, smirking with obvious relish.

'Pinning a badge on a turd don't make that turd a sheriff.'

As the men around him grunted a laugh, Curtis gritted his teeth.

'You can't speak to me like that no more,' he muttered, bunching his fists.

'Mayor Ellison once told me it wasn't fitting for two lawmen to brawl in public.' Lincoln looked Curtis up and down. 'But that's no problem, seeing as you ain't a real lawman.'

Curtis rocked forward, seemingly ready to take out his anger on Lincoln, but then outside a gunshot ripped out. Within the saloon there was the usual combination of people moving towards the window to see what had happened combined with others moving away to avoid being caught in any cross-fire.

Lincoln roughly bundled Curtis aside, then pushed customers away to reach the batwings. He saw that the incident was already over. A lone man lay crumpled in a heap in the road, facing away from Lincoln, his legs drawn up to his chest.

Lincoln issued a quick order for everyone to stay inside, then headed outside. He looked up and down the road. Few people were outside and all of them were gravitating towards the body with none of them holding a drawn gun. Neither was anybody moving away from the body.

Lincoln would question the witnesses later, but as he approached the body he winced. It was Judge Murphy. He ran, then skidded to a halt beside the body, seeing that Murphy was clutching a smoking gun. He knelt and rolled him over to find that Murphy was still breathing, but only shallowly. He looked up at Lincoln with glazed eyes.

'Who?' Lincoln asked.

'Me,' Murphy said, his voice weak and barely audible. 'I guess I've had so much whiskey I can't even shoot myself right.'

Murphy let the gun fall from his grasp, then moved for his jacket, but he was too weak to do whatever action he'd been trying to perform. His hand dropped and his head lolled. Lincoln looked over his shoulder and saw Curtis pacing towards him. He turned back and completed Murphy's movement by moving his jacket aside. Sticking out of his inside pocket was a photograph.

Lincoln didn't need to examine it to know what it was but he still quickly pocketed the picture, then turned to face the advancing Curtis.

'Step away from him,' Curtis said.

'He shot himself.' Lincoln backed away a pace.

'That's what you would say, but now I'm back in town I'll work that out for myself.'

As Curtis moved in and bent over Murphy's body Lincoln backed away. He watched the crowd moving in towards them, noting that many people were eyeing him with suspicion. Then he flinched in surprise when a hand clutched his shoulder, halting him.

'Leave while you still can,' a voice whispered in his ear.

Lincoln glanced back, seeing Jack Porter standing behind him.

'I'm staying to sort this out.'

'Don't,' Jack urged. 'You know the way Sheriff Curtis works. He'll need someone to blame for that death, and you know how much he hates you.'

'I was in the saloon with dozens of witnesses. Even he wouldn't try to twist the truth that much.'

Jack shrugged then turned away to head down the road.

'Then I'll leave you to your fate.' He stopped for a moment. 'As it appears you don't want to hear the truth.'

Lincoln was minded not to follow him, but he saw Curtis cast a suspicious glance at him, then beckon one of the hired guns to come closer so he could talk to him. With much nodding and waving in Lincoln's directions, Curtis issued the man with his orders, and Lincoln had no doubt that Jack was right about their nature. So Lincoln slipped into the gathering crowd, and hurried after Jack, catching up with him after a dozen quick strides.

Jack merely glanced at him and smiled as if he'd known all along that Lincoln would come with him.

'And what is the truth?' Lincoln asked.

'I know who killed Ben Pringle.' Jack raised a hand as Lincoln asked for a name, then pointed ahead to the stables. 'But only when we can't be seen or heard.'

Lincoln complied with Jack's wishes and stayed quiet until they reached the stables. He took a quick glance around the stalls confirming that nobody was inside, then turned to Jack.

'All right,' he said, 'tell me what you know.'

'It's a long story.'

'Then shorten it. I have to deal with Curtis before he gets the chance to deal with me.'

Jack nodded and started walking in small circles, rubbing his chin and looking as if he was arranging his thoughts. Lincoln tapped a foot on the ground as he bided his time. His patience had worn thin and he was about to demand that Jack hurry up and talk when a creak sounded behind him. Lincoln swirled round, seeing a man holding a sack leap out at him from the shadows. He raised his hands to ward the person off, but the man slammed into him and with a leading shoulder barged him to his knees.

The sack tore down over his head and shoulders and firm hands pinned his arms to his side. His assailant then wrapped an arm around his neck and attempted to wrestle him to the ground, but Lincoln kicked out and managed to loop a leg around the man's ankle. He pulled back, tugging the man over, then grabbed the sack, aiming to tear it away, but a rope then landed over his head and pulled tight around his chest, securing the sack in place.

Several sets of footsteps stomped around him, giving Lincoln the impression that he was now surrounded. Sure enough a solid blow from a stick thwacked into his back, making him stumble forward. A second blow to the back of the head sent him to his knees.

Groggily he tried to right himself, but hands then splayed all over him, ropes were pulled tight around his legs, stomach, and another around his chest. A man shouted out instructions for how they should secure him and Lincoln recognized Karl Humboldt's voice. He also guessed that the other man was the remaining Humboldt brother. Worse, any hope that Jack Porter would come to his aid fled when he heard Jack speak up.

'I told you I could get him here,' he said.

‘What you want in payment?’ Karl asked.

‘Nothing other than the first punch before you deal with him.’

Karl chuckled. ‘I reckon that sounds like a fair deal.’

When they’d trussed him up, they dragged him to a horse and bundled him over it, then mounted up and headed outside. Lincoln listened, hoping to hear someone sound an alarm on seeing the group head out of town – he even wouldn’t have minded if that person was Sheriff Curtis – but he heard nothing. So he had no choice but to settle down to suffering a journey to wherever they were taking him.

He judged that a half-hour passed before the group came to a halt. Around him he heard the men dismount then Karl tipped him off the back of the horse.

The river was gurgling close by and he guessed they’d brought him to a private location, perhaps close to the spot where he’d found Sheckley Dolby’s body last week. He also surmised that they intended to dispose of his body by depositing him in the water.

Karl tugged the sack from his head, and Lincoln saw that he did face the two Humboldt brothers along with Jack Porter.

‘Can I kill him now?’ Heinrich Humboldt

asked, grinning as he paced up to Lincoln.

'No,' Karl said. 'Move out the way. I want to rough him up first.'

Karl moved past Heinrich with his fist raised, but Jack spoke up.

'Wait,' he said. 'You agreed I'd get the first punch.'

Karl shrugged then feigned swinging a punch at Lincoln. Despite Lincoln's determination to avoid reacting, it still made him flinch away. Karl laughed then stood aside with an eager gleam lighting his eyes as he ensured he was in the best position to watch the punishment Jack delivered.

Jack wasted no time in pacing up to him and without preamble rocked back his arm. He thundered a low fist into Lincoln's chest, the blow sending a bolt of pain lancing through his ribs and bending him double. Then he raised a foot and with his heel pushed Lincoln over onto his side.

'That satisfy you?' Karl asked.

'Not yet,' Jack muttered then took a run at Lincoln and kicked him deep in the guts, blasting all the air from Lincoln's chest and making him roll over twice before he came to a shuddering and painful halt. 'Although that should be enough. Now you can make him suffer.'

'I intend to,' Karl said, cracking his knuckles and advancing on Lincoln. 'He'll be begging me to let Heinrich kill him before the night is over.'

Jack snorted then shook his head. 'Don't just make him suffer with your fists. Tear him up inside.'

Karl halted. 'What you mean?'

'I mean tell him the truth. Tell him what you did to Sheriff Ben Pringle before you finish him off. That'll ruin him more than any amount of blows.'

Karl chuckled. 'I guess telling him that would be fun. He's spent all that time searching for the man who killed the lawman and he was right here all along.'

Lincoln twisted and managed to roll himself over. He looked up at the three men.

'You and your brothers killed him?' he asked.

'Yeah,' Karl said, grinning. 'He'd been tearing himself up about something for months and he thought I was behind it, but I wasn't. I'd had enough of him pulling me in all the time so I shot him up.'

'And Wesley Jameson?'

Karl shook his head as he advanced on Lincoln with his fist raised.

'You don't ask the questions. I get to ask

them.' He glanced at his fist. 'And this will do my talking for me.'

Karl took another pace towards him and despite the urge to roll away, Lincoln glared up defiantly at him. To Karl's side, Heinrich paced in, while over Karl's shoulder Lincoln saw Jack also move in. Lincoln looked at each man in turn, wondering which one of them would attack him first, but to his surprise he saw Jack slip his gun from its holster. Lincoln looked away from him, hope flickering in his mind as to what he was doing, but he was not wanting to alert the brothers.

He watched the advancing Karl and when Karl beckoned to Heinrich for him to drag Lincoln to his feet, Jack fired, blasting Heinrich in the side and sending him tumbling away. Then he swung his gun round to aim at Karl, who was turning at the hip, his gun coming to hand, but he was already too late. A single gunshot tore the gun from his hand. Then Jack advanced on Karl with his gun now aimed at Karl's head.

Karl stood before him, his stance uncertain as he darted his gaze back and forth between Jack and his dead brother. When Jack signified that he get down on his knees, Karl complied.

'What you turn on us for?' he whined.

'I got arrested because Lincoln reckoned I was behind the crimes you committed. I've now cleared my name. Now, if you want to live, tell Lincoln what you did to Jameson.'

'We did nothing.'

'But you burn down the saloon when you thought Wesley wouldn't give you an alibi.'

'Alex did do that, but only because this man paid him to do it. None of us actually killed him.'

Jack stood over Karl and placed the barrel of the gun against his forehead.

'Admit the truth.'

'That is the truth!'

'Jack,' Lincoln urged, 'evidence gained under these circumstances don't count for much.'

'Who cares about evidence?' Jack snapped. 'I just want the truth.'

'But... But...' Karl spluttered, 'I didn't kill Wesley Jameson, only Sheriff Pringle.'

'That's your final word?'

'Yeah.'

Jack shrugged then fired, kicking Karl's body away and to the ground. Lincoln watched the body roll to a halt, feeling no satisfaction in seeing the killer of his old friend meeting his end this way, then he looked at Jack.

'That was wrong,' he said. 'You push 'em to the brink to get 'em to talk, but you don't kill 'em.'

'I guess that means I won't ever make a lawman, then.' Jack holstered his gun and offered a smile. 'So have you got a problem with what I had to do?'

'The situation was fraught. You did what you had to do.' Lincoln flexed his chest. 'I just hope for your sake you didn't bust my ribs while you did it.'

'So,' Lincoln said, 'you haven't left here in a week?'

Mayor Ellison looked up from his desk. He was haggard, his clothes ruffled and slept-in, the rank smell in the office suggesting he really hadn't left here since Lincoln had headed off to Black Point. He glanced at Lincoln's companion Jack, then back to Lincoln.

'I haven't,' he said, his voice gruff and defeated. 'Not while someone is out there waiting for us.'

'There's one less of the seven now.' Lincoln waited for Ellison to react, but he just looked back at him with blank eyes. 'Judge Murphy is dead.'

'I heard the gunshot... Did you see who did it?'

'He did it to himself, like all the others have thought of doing in their darkest hours, except he had the guts to pull the trigger.'

Ellison shot a glance at the top drawer of his desk, his guilty expression suggesting he had also considered that option.

'Or he'd had so much whiskey he didn't know what he was doing no more.'

'Or that.' Lincoln provided a grim smile. 'But Sheriff Curtis is now in charge of the investigation so you have nothing to worry about.'

Ellison snorted. 'I gather from your tone that you don't approve of my decision to make him a sheriff.'

'Nope, but that doesn't matter to me. My time here is over. You called me in to find out who killed Ben Pringle and I did. It was Karl Humboldt, aided by his brothers.'

'But they didn't kill the others?'

'Nope.'

Ellison got to his feet and came out from behind his desk to face Lincoln.

'Then you have to stay to work out the rest.'

'I don't. There is no connection between Karl killing Ben and the recent killings of everyone in that photograph.' Lincoln smiled when Ellison flinched. 'Yes, I have seen the picture. I even have several copies of it. Perhaps I'll give them to Sheriff Curtis before I leave. It might help him work out what's happening before the killer gets you and Billy Stone.'

'Don't go.' Ellison dropped to his knees and in a parody of pleading held his hands out beseechingly and without pride. He even looked at Jack as if he might help him. 'Please.'

Lincoln considered this once proud man, shaking his head in disbelief.

'Perhaps the killer won't bother killing you. You're a destroyed man already.' Lincoln turned away, fully intending to leave and not look back, but then a sudden thought came to him and he turned back. 'How is Billy Stone?'

'Billy is fine. He's looking into several ventures already. Nothing depresses him. He's been bankrupt before and he'll probably get it all back before he loses it all again.'

Lincoln nodded, sudden understanding coming to him.

'Then he'll survive, even if you won't.'

'What you mean?'

'I mean I know what the killer is doing.' Lincoln glanced at Jack. 'And I know who he is.'

CHAPTER 12

'When are you going to tell us why you brought us here?' Mayor Ellison asked.

Lincoln didn't reply immediately as he paced away from Destitution's saloon to stand before the three gravestones. He stood with them at his back then looked at his assembled group of Jack Porter, Mayor Ellison, Billy Stone and Sheriff Curtis.

'Five people who were in this picture are now dead.' Lincoln withdrew the picture from his pocket and held it aloft. 'A hounded Sheriff Ben Pringle died at Karl Humboldt's hands, although that wasn't how it was supposed to end for him. Wesley died after his saloon burnt down, Sheckley died after discovering the woman he'd fallen for gave her favours to everyone who passed through, and Lenox died after discovering the same truth. Judge Murphy died yesterday after losing the faith of the townsfolk. That just leaves you two alive out of the original seven, one because you hid in your offices, and the other because you're in a good mood.'

Billy laughed. 'I guess I am irrepressible, but why would that keep me alive?'

'It only takes a bullet to kill a man, but if you're after revenge maybe for some people that's not enough. Whoever killed them wanted something more. He wanted to break them first.'

'Then who is doing it?' Ellison asked.

'You two know already, or at least suspect, and it all depends on the fact that this photograph has a date on it that's before the date on those graves.'

'That could be a mistake,' the mayor said, not meeting Lincoln's eye.

'Perhaps, but I prefer a simpler explanation. Quincy Allen was the man they couldn't hang and the trouble with boasts like that is they're a challenge, and so you decided to hang him anyhow. You couldn't find a witness to his crimes who was brave enough to talk, so you invented a crime.'

'He shot his brothers,' Billy murmured with a shame-faced glance at Ellison.

'He did shoot three of them, according to you, but I'm saying the truth is you invented a crime, sentenced him, then hanged him. Later, his brothers came looking for revenge and you killed them, then claimed that that was the crime you hanged him for. Nobody questioned your story when it was Quincy Allen who'd died and you had the bodies and you had the photograph to prove it.'

'You can't prove that,' Ellison said with an imploring glance at Sheriff Curtis, although the strangely quiet Curtis didn't return that glance.

'I can't,' Lincoln said, 'not now the witness, the lawman, the bounty hunter, the judge, and the executioner are all dead, and if you two want to take that secret to the grave, you can. Trouble is, that might be closer than you hope it'll be because the one man you didn't silence is now taking his revenge.

'Who?'

Lincoln paced up to the line of men and stood before Ellison.

'Three brothers came looking for you, but the fourth stayed behind.'

'But he was only a kid.'

'Yeah, but ten years on, he ain't a kid no more. Can you even remember his name?'

'No.'

Lincoln turned away from Ellison then paced down the line of men until he stood before Jack, who was watching proceedings quietly but intently.

'What about you, Jack?' Lincoln asked.

'Do you know the name of this youngest brother?'

'No,' Jack said, his tone unconcerned.

'Then guess.'

'I believe you reckon his name was...' Jack rubbed his chin, then winked. '...was Jack.'

Lincoln smiled. 'I do.'

'You could be right, but if so, it's a coincidence.'

'That would be one coincidence too many.'

'Maybe, but why did you have to bring us all the way out here to present your coincidence?'

'Because Destitution is where it all started, and it must conjure up memories for everyone who was involved, no matter how inscrutable a poker-face those men put on.'

'Not for me it doesn't,' Jack said, shrugging. 'I've never been here before.'

'You came here ten years ago, except you were too young to help your brothers. And you were here this week, and you were old enough to help me.'

For the first time Jack looked away. 'Why would I want to do that?'

'I don't know, but before you tell me why, I'll give you a tour of the town where these men hanged your brother then killed your other brothers when they came looking for revenge.'

Jack snorted. 'You got this wrong.'

'You sure did,' Curtis said, speaking for the first time since arriving in Destitution. 'If anyone arrests Jack, it'll be me. You won't question him no more.'

Curtis walked behind Ellison and Billy and placed a hand on Jack's shoulder. He moved to shepherd him away, but to Lincoln's surprise, Jack squirmed away then turned to face the saloon.

'I have nothing to fear from Lincoln's ridiculous accusation. I am not Quincy Allen's brother and being here doesn't concern me.' He walked towards the saloon and stood looking at it. 'Where did they hang him?'

'You can tell from this.' Lincoln joined Jack and gave him the picture. Jack glanced from it to the saloon and back, then moved a few paces to the side.

'I believe it would be there,' he said, pointing to a spot beside the door.

Lincoln looked back at Billy and Ellison and received a shamefaced nod from Ellison. Billy lowered his head and wouldn't meet his eye. Curtis hadn't followed them: he had also lowered his head and wasn't looking at the saloon.

Lincoln beckoned for Billy and Ellison to join him and reluctantly they came over. The four men stood in a line looking at the saloon. It was now so peaceful and the saloon was such a wreck that Lincoln couldn't imagine that the scene the photograph depicted had actually happened here. But he hoped that those who had been here would be able to envisage it, and the guilty ought to react.

Unfortunately, the minimal reactions Lincoln saw didn't help him. Billy shuffled from foot to foot, Ellison frowned, and Jack, consummate poker-player that he was, looked at the saloon with the hint of a smile on his lips. To try to force some sort of reaction Lincoln beckoned for the argumentative Curtis to join them, but Curtis was glaring at the backs of the line of men and ignored him.

'Come on, Alan,' Lincoln said. 'Be useful for once in your miserable existence and see if you can help jog these people's consciences.'

'I ain't going to,' Curtis spat out, his eyes flaring, 'and the sooner we leave, the sooner I can start a proper investigation.'

'I just want everyone to remember the details of what happened here when a man died swinging on the end of the rope for no crime.'

Curtis swore and bunched his jaw, his anger out of all proportion to Lincoln's request. Lincoln was pondering on the reason for that anger when Ellison spoke up.

'Quincy Allen committed plenty of crimes,' he said. 'He deserved what happened to him.'

This was the sort of comment Lincoln had hoped to hear when he'd decided to bring everyone here and while he replied he looked at Jack.

'And his brothers?'

'They were as bad as he was.'

'Then show me where you killed them.'

'Won't do no good. They were all worthless varmints and everybody breathed easier after we'd disposed of them.'

Ellison set his feet wide, gathering his courage and defying Lincoln to argue with him, while Jack swung round to look at Lincoln, his lively eyes and smile suggesting he knew Lincoln was looking for a reaction in him. Then his smile died and he flinched to look behind them at Curtis. Lincoln moved too and saw that while they'd been talking Curtis had drawn his gun. Lincoln started to ask why he'd done that but he received his answer in the worst possible way when Curtis fired.

He blasted a slug into Billy's back, throwing him on his front, then swung his gun on to Ellison. Jack saw what he was about to do and pushed Ellison away, his sudden action saving the mayor from getting a bullet in the centre of his back; instead the slug caught him through the side and sent him spinning.

Lincoln drew his gun and in a fluid motion turned at the hip. Curtis was now running for the trading post beside the saloon and Lincoln's shot winged past his shoulder. Then Jack and the stumbling Ellison blocked his line of sight.

Curtis hurled himself through the doorway. The moment he disappeared from view Lincoln ordered Jack to get Ellison into the saloon. Then he dropped to one knee and checked on Billy, but the man was already still. So Lincoln hurried after the two men and into the saloon.

Jack helped Ellison to sit beside the door, but when he released him Ellison rolled to the side and lay on the floor. His breathing was shallow as he looked up at Lincoln.

'It would seem you were right,' he murmured. 'Curtis wasn't the right man to be sheriff.'

'Glad you realized, but did I work out what happened here right?'

'Yeah.'

'And what was that younger brother's name?'

'I can't remember, honestly.'

'Alan, perhaps,' Jack said, standing behind him, 'or maybe even Curtis, as in not Alan Curtis, but Curtis Allen.'

Ellison shook his head weakly. 'I can't remember.'

'But it's a reasonable assumption,' Lincoln said. 'Curtis was nearby when Wesley was murdered and he wasn't in town for the last few days.'

'You can't worry about that now,' Jack said. 'He's hiding in the trading post and it'll take some doing to get him out of somewhere with so many hiding-places.'

Lincoln frowned. 'It's odd how you know so much about the building next door. Time to tell the truth, Jack.'

Jack sighed and spread his hands. 'I was here recently, as you know.'

'You killed Wilhelm Humboldt?'

'And saved your life.'

'Why?'

'Because you were convinced I'd killed Sheriff Pringle and exposing the real killer was the only way I could clear my name.'

Lincoln nodded. Wilhelm had said the man who killed him was death, but Lincoln now reckoned this was just a statement from a dying man rather than identifying Jack as being the masked man.

'I believe you. Now stay here and look after the mayor.' Lincoln raised a hand when Jack started to object. 'I wouldn't be a lawman if I endangered an innocent bystander.'

Jack acknowledged Lincoln's admittance of his innocence with a curt nod, then knelt beside Ellison and laid a comforting hand on his shoulder. Lincoln slipped through the doorway and slowly walked along beside the saloon, keeping the trading post ahead in view. He had a good view of the window and door and he looked back and forth between them as he approached.

He was five yards away when the low sun caught the glint of something metallic protruding from the wall. In a sudden shocked moment Lincoln realized that it was a gun barrel poking out through a gap in the wall. He dived towards the saloon wall a moment before Curtis fired, the bullet whining past him. Lincoln rolled and came to a halt slammed up against the wall.

'Good try, Curtis,' Lincoln said. 'You just

wasted your only chance.'

'I'll still get you,' Curtis shouted from inside the post.

'Why have you been so determined to kill me? I had nothing to do with what happened to your brothers.'

'The lawman got away when Karl Humboldt got him before I did. I'd spent months ruining his life but luckily I'm not too particular. As long as I get to kill a lawman, I'm happy.'

'Then you'll fail.' Lincoln slowly got to his feet. 'But before we end this, tell me one thing – what really happened to your brothers ten years ago? I'll make sure everyone knows after I've killed you.'

Curtis snorted and for a moment Lincoln thought he wouldn't answer. But then he began speaking, telling Lincoln of how his brothers had left for Destitution, looking for revenge and leaving him behind.

As promised, Lincoln listened to the tale as he walked along, keeping his back to the wall. He ducked into the space between the saloon and the trading post. Then as silently as possible he headed to the back of the building.

Curtis was still speaking, his voice wistful as he described the events that had shaped his life and led him on his quest for revenge. For the first time Lincoln let himself feel a twinge of empathy for Curtis's predicament as he paced along the back of the post.

That didn't change his resolution to end this now, and with a quiet but firm movement he stepped to the side to stand in the open doorway. Curtis's voice had allowed him to locate his position in the post and he immediately picked out the shape of the man kneeling beside the front window.

But Curtis was looking directly at him with his gun already drawn and aimed at him.

Lincoln hurled himself to the side, firing in midair. Curtis fired at the same moment. Lincoln felt Curtis's slug tear across his sleeve, but Lincoln's aim was better, slamming high into Curtis's shoulder and standing him straight before he tumbled out through the window.

Lincoln hit the floor on his side, skidded to a halt, then jumped to his feet and hurried to the window, aiming to finish off Curtis before he got the chance to get his senses about him. He looked outside, but then darted back as a bullet thudded into the sill, sending splinters flying.

Worse, in his quick glance he hadn't been

able to see Curtis.

Another gunshot sounded followed by a returning shot as Curtis traded gunfire with, presumably, Jack Porter. Lincoln wasted no time and charged out through the door, looking towards the saloon as he guessed that Curtis would have gone in that direction. Curtis wasn't visible.

Lincoln still kept running while darting his gaze around, then saw Jack step out through the saloon doorway, and he was pointing over Lincoln's shoulder.

'Over there!' he shouted.

Lincoln put his trust in Jack's honesty and dropped to one knee. He fired on the turn, sighting Curtis as he completed his turn. His first shot was wild, so he threw himself to the ground. He rolled and came to rest on his side with his gun thrust out and aimed up at Curtis.

In response, Curtis swung his gun to the side to follow Lincoln's tumbling form, but a moment before he could fire, Lincoln pulled the trigger.

His slug caught Curtis low in the chest, bending him double and forcing him to step backwards. Curtis still managed to right himself and with his teeth gritted forced himself to raise his gun, but two shots hammered into him. One slug came from Lincoln catching him high in the chest and a second from Jack tore into his side.

And so Sheriff Alan Curtis, or Curtis Allen as he used to be known, went tumbling, and this time he didn't get up again.

EPILOGUE

'Obliged for your help, Jack,' Lincoln said.

He was standing before the grave of Sheriff Ben Pringle with Jack standing a respectful two paces behind him.

'It was the least I could do,' Jack said. He provided a hollow laugh. 'Curtis was determined that a lawman should die. At least the right one did.'

'Not true. Curtis was no lawman.'

Jack nodded then lowered his head for a suitable length of time.

'Do we have a problem?' he said.

'Nope.'

'Then I'll leave you with your friend.' Jack paced forward to look down at the grave. He looked at it for several seconds before smiling to Lincoln, which Lincoln acknowledged. Then he left.

As he listened to Jack mount his horse and leave, Lincoln searched again for the right words to say before he too left.

He had to accept that Alan Curtis had got everything he'd wanted when he'd set out to get his revenge on everyone who had wiped out his brothers ten years ago. With the mayor dying earlier, despite Doc Thoreau's efforts, all his targets were now dead, and every one of them had suffered and had had cause to remember, reflect and regret what they'd done before they'd died.

Despite his abhorrence of people like Curtis and his brothers, Lincoln couldn't help but think it was justice of a kind.

Earlier today Lincoln had cleared up the last of the loose ends when he'd found a mask in the shape of a skull in Curtis's desk – his disguise while carrying out his revenge. With even Alex Humboldt's role in Ben's demise now providing a justification for his hanging, Lincoln could leave town with his own conscience clear.

A light rain was in the air and the wind was rustling the dust past him as Lincoln withdrew the photographs he'd collected from the various victims.

'Ben, you forgot your duty ten years ago,' Lincoln said, finding at last that he could say the words, 'but that doesn't make you a bad man.'

One at a time he tore the photographs into pieces. Then he scattered the fragments to the wind, turned and left the graveside.

When he rode away from Ben's house he kept beside the river and headed north towards Black Point. His destination was a small trading post run by Sarah Devere, one of the many good things in life he had in common with his old friend.